ALICE &

NATALIE KLEINMAN

AFTER ALL THESE YEARS

Complete and Unabridged

LINFORD
Leicester

First published in Great Britain in 2014

First Linford Edition
published 2015

A catalogue record for this book is available
from the British Library.

ISBN 978–1–4448–2550–3

Published by
F. A. Thorpe (Publishing)
Anstey, Leicestershire

Set by Words & Graphics Ltd.
Anstey, Leicestershire
Printed and bound in Great Britain by
T. J. International Ltd., Padstow, Cornwall

This book is printed on acid-free paper

1

Honey was standing behind the counter absent-mindedly moving around the display of cakes and thinking about her mother when someone tugged at the doorbell. She looked up to see a ghost from the past.

'Guy! What on earth are you doing here?'

The smile that had caused her toes to curl all those years ago had lost none of its power to charm. The boy had become a man. He'd always been tall, but now the body had filled out to fit the frame and it was a muscled giant she saw before her, his jeans and sweater well-fitting enough to show the evidence.

'Not the reception I was hoping for, Honeysuckle. The prodigal son I'm not, but I expected at least a hug from an old friend.'

'Old indeed. It's been, what, close on fourteen years!' she said, when in fact she knew to the day how long it was. She found herself engulfed in an embrace she'd spent most of her teenage years dreaming about. 'What brings you back to Rills Ford after all this time? I thought you'd left the rustic country town behind you.'

'I'm here on business partly, and partly for pleasure. I've missed the old place. Didn't Bas tell you I was coming?' he said, raising one eyebrow quizzically in a way which brought youthful memories flooding back.

'Not a word. Did you have a good time in Australia?'

'It was great. Hard graft, but I enjoyed designing the building. All glass and angular sections. It's a modern arts centre and I'd love to see it when it's finished but I'll have to make do with the video. There's far too much I want to do here.'

'I'd love to be able to see a bit of the world. Not much chance of that at the

2

moment though.'

There was a pause until Guy remembered he'd been charged with a message. 'Bas asked me to pass this on to you, by the way, to give to your mother,' he said, handing her a photo of the five-year-old nephew she'd never met under which was written in spidery letters, 'To Gran with love from Tom'. 'He was hoping it would mean something to her. He told me . . . He thought, well, that since her fall she's become a little confused; that . . . ' Not quite sure how to continue, Guy left the rest of the sentence hanging in the air.

Honey was focusing on how much her mother had lost. With Daisy's disability had come a lack of independence and Honey, her mother's daughter to her fingertips, had taken the tough decision to agree that she would be better off in a care home than in the cramped living premises of the Honey Bun Tearooms. The suggestion had come from Daisy herself. Ever pragmatic, she'd said, 'I think it's probably time I went and mixed with people my own age. I know several of the residents at the Grange and I'm no use to you here anymore.' There was no self-pity in the statement. To her it was a matter of fact. A broken leg and a fractured wrist had left her pretty much helpless. Her confusion was sporadic and, the doctors had said, probably the result of trauma. It was to be hoped it would pass as quickly as the time it would take for broken bones to mend. In the meantime she professed to be loving every moment she was being spoiled.

Honey dragged her thoughts away from her mother and looked up at Guy. 'Look, why don't you sit down. I'll make you a cup of tea.'

'Now I know I'm home. The Englishman's answer to all problems — a cup of tea.'

'English *man*?' she couldn't resist asking, a little archly and completely out of character. He'd always had the power to rob her of her ease.

4

'It was a figure of speech.'

Honey wasn't sure if he was laughing at her, but she was glad to have something to occupy her hands, though she was doubtful of her ability to prevent the tea spilling into the saucer. She overcame the problem by making it in a pot. Guy was peering at the counter, inspecting the array of cakes.

'Do you make all these yourself? Any chance I could have a piece of chocolate fudge?' he asked disarmingly.

'Yes I do, and of course you can.'

By the time they sat down Honey had regained some of her composure. Guy looked around. 'It's exactly as I remember it, even down to the prints on the walls. Except this. I don't remember this,' he said, pouring himself a cup and running his thumb over the bee logo on the teapot, then sucking it because it was hot. 'Your idea?'

'Yes.'

'I like it, and that you've carried it throughout, even down to the serviettes.'

Honey warmed to his praise. 'Thank you. But you're right about the rest, although the walls do get painted regularly; the same colours though. People like continuity.'

'I've always liked change.'

Didn't she know it! She remembered the stream of girlfriends that had passed through his hands. Basil had been good at keeping his sister updated. Much as she'd longed to, she'd never been one of their number. She pushed the thought away and tried to concentrate on what Guy was saying.

'I stuck with the name though. Somehow I never got around to changing that and in its way it's been quite useful in business. Once they've heard it, no one's likely to forget.'

'That's for sure. Everyone knows Guy Fawkes, even if you do spell it differently.'

They both smiled, remembering the bond that had held the three of them together: Honey, her brother and his best friend. It wasn't as bad for Honey and Basil. Only Guy had ever called her Honeysuckle, and only to tease. Basil didn't really mind his name, though in any case most people called him Bas. But Guy . . . Somehow he could never forgive whatever evil genius had prompted his parents to saddle him with a name that summoned up thoughts of bonfires and fireworks. Early November was never a great time for him. Of course they couldn't help their surname. He knew that, but he couldn't help feeling that something like Harry would have been better.

'Is there a Mrs Ffoulkes?' Honey asked, though she already knew the answer. She'd followed his career through the eyes of her brother and online.

'No. Those first few years I was too busy making my fortune.' He meant it, literally. Guy was a hugely successful, internationally famous architect, most of his work looking as if it came from some futuristic film. He was represented in many of the capital cities around the world. 'I've had the odd fling, but I've never found what Basil and Lucy have.'

Honey didn't think he sounded too distressed, and Basil had reported many 'odd flings' over the years. Certainly it would appear Guy had not been lonely.

'What about you? Is there a Mr Bunting?'

Obviously I was never part of Bas and Guy's conversations, or he would know that already. 'No. As you know, Dad died three years after you and Bas went to uni. Mum lost interest in the tearooms — totally out of character — and it was even harder to get away. Not that I wanted to. I love it here,' she said, sounding defensive though she hadn't meant to. 'Anyway, Mr Right hasn't walked through the door yet.'

This wasn't strictly true. Her Mr Right had come through the door barely half an hour ago, though she'd known it was him when she'd waved him off as a love-struck sixteen-year-old. She'd cried herself to sleep many times. She'd have been glad to know he'd never suspected, but then he never had seen her as anyone other than Bas's scruffy little sister. Nowadays her auburn curls were under control, pulled back under a chic mob cap because she worked with food but in a way that flattered her elfin face. At other times she let them fall free on her shoulders, swinging as she walked in a way that made heads turn to follow her progress down the street. A smart black dress had taken the place of a rather unflattering school uniform and the baggy leisure clothes she'd worn to hide her burgeoning figure, now slimmed down to a rather attractive size 10, perfect for a woman of 5′ 8″. She was hoping he'd noticed that much at least.

'Well, you're looking good.' *He'd noticed*. 'So I wouldn't give up yet.'

'Does anyone ever give up? Have you?'

'I'm not sure anyone would have me. I'm not easy to live with, as any of my ex-girlfriends would vouch for, I'm sure.' He changed the subject, somewhat abruptly it seemed to Honey. 'So how bad is your mother?'

'At the moment she's a bit mixed up, but it's been a lot for her to take in. The accident, the total change of lifestyle. She's been trying to help me here since I took over from her but like I said, since Dad passed away, her heart hasn't been in it. Frankly the move to the Grange has been wonderful for her. It's been years since I've seen her this contented.'

'I can't believe it! I remember sneaking in here; confiding in her; tasting her chocolate fudge cake which, by the way, was in no way superior to yours — and I always thought hers was great.'

She leaned across the table and wiped the corner of his mouth with a serviette. 'Thank you, but you're supposed to put it in your mouth,' she said, smiling.

He raised his own napkin as she withdrew hers and their hands touched briefly. Guy seemed not to notice Honey's confusion.

'She was always a great listener as well as a great talker. I'm sure half of Rills Ford confided in her.'

'Why don't you come and visit with me? You never know; it might trigger some memories.'

'Well, if you think it'll help, I'd love to see her. I'll do anything I can. I still remember how good she was to me. There was always an extra hug, and I wasn't the only one either. We kids would be falling over ourselves to see her, and not just for her cake.'

Honey struggled to cope with the lump in her throat that these memories had brought back. The teashop had been a magnet for all generations.

'Don't be upset if she doesn't recognise you. Like I said, she's a bit confused at the moment. Mind you, you might be just what she needs.'

'In that case I'll pop in when I leave here. I don't suppose you can come right now?'

'No, but I go every evening after I close the shop.'

'Shall I wait till later, then? Does six thirty suit you? If you're free maybe we could have dinner.'

Honey managed not to squeak. She told herself the invitation was only offered because he was at a loose end, but there were some things it was better not to be too proud about.

'That would be lovely.'

'Daisy might not give me a hug like she used to, but it will be enough if she holds my hand; even better if she gives it a squeeze. She always knew how to make us all feel good, whereas my mother . . . well, let's just say she knew her place.'

'Several rungs up the ladder from the rest of us mere mortals.'

'Oh yes. 'Choose your friends wisely,' she said to me. I was never in any doubt as to what she meant by that. Bas and I laughed about it all the time. She wasn't too keen that I spent most of my time with the scruffiest boy in the school and his equally scruffy little sister.'

Honey bristled slightly. It was all right for her to describe herself that way, but she didn't like it from Guy. She did feel sorry for him though. Mrs Ffoulkes wasn't a warm woman. No one had missed her or her husband when they left Rills Ford. It was unanimously agreed in the town that the Grange was being put to far better use nowadays.

'Do they like living abroad?'

'Are you kidding? A villa; staff; wonderful weather and nothing to do but worry about whether her nail varnish is chipped?'

'And your father?'

'Does as he's told. Always has. What about you, Honeysuckle? It's been your life then, this little town in middle England?'

'Don't knock it, Guy,' Honey replied with a definite edge to her voice. 'I'm perfectly contented here. I can think of worse places to live.'

'Oh, I wasn't knocking it at all. It's a wonderful town. I meant it when I said I'd come home partly for reasons of pleasure.' Honey was pleased he still regarded it as home. 'The pleasure will be restoring my old home and making it suitable to live in. I've had enough of change. I want to come back to my roots.'

'Your old home! But you can't! People are living there. You can't just throw them out.'

'That's where the business part comes in,' he said excitedly, not realising how he'd upset her. 'I've designed a new care home which I'd like to build in the grounds of the Grange. As soon as it's finished the residents can move across and I'll start renovating the house. The facilities will be much better than they are now — in both places.'

'You can't,' she repeated, this time raising her voice. 'My mother lives there. What gives you the right to mess with people's lives like that?'

14

She saw him stiffen; didn't care. All she could think about was the plight of the residents. *Doesn't he have any idea what it's like? Any change in routine could be catastrophic. Does he really think he can come back here after all this time and turn everything upside-down?*

'The right? It's mine. I own it. So if you'll pardon me, I'll do what I damned well please.'

2

Guy tried to calm down as he walked the mile and a half back to the Grange, but he wasn't used to being crossed in quite such a forthright manner. The truth was he was stung by Honey's reaction. Following his success and the accumulation of an almost indecent amount of wealth, he'd turned his hand to what he thought of as giving something back. *It isn't as if I wanted a pat on the back. She didn't have to be quite so aggressive.* In fact his philanthropic projects were always anonymous because that was the way he preferred it. It was true he wanted to settle again in Rills Ford. It was true he wanted his family home back. He knew *as Honey would if only she were honest* that the Grange wasn't best suited to be a care home. *I wonder if she knows it was me who gave consent*

16

in the first place. Or did she believe my mother had suddenly undergone a surge of altruism and allowed her old home to be used in such a manner?

Guy had bought the Grange from his parents some years ago, partially to fund their move and partly because he'd always had the intention of returning to his corner of England where as a child, and in spite of his mother, he'd been happy. He looked around him now and was more than ever conscious of how much he'd missed the place. Even in February the bare trees added a gentleness to the quaint architecture that was prevalent in this part of the country, and the golden-coloured stonework that formed the structure of the buildings reflected warmth in the winter sun.

'Guy — Guy Ffoulkes! Would you look at you now. I nearly didn't recognise you.'

He looked down at the old lady standing on the pavement directly in his path and whom he'd almost mowed down, distracted as he was by his surroundings and his memories.

'Hello, Mrs Worthington. It's nice to see you again.'

Guy realised there were going to be a lot of surprised people and he would probably have to go through this ritual several times in the next few days.

'Whatever brings you back to Rills Ford? We all thought you'd gone for good.'

'And glad of it, I expect, eh?'

'No, no. It wasn't you.'

Mrs Worthington realised the implication of what she'd said and had the grace to blush. There weren't many who'd liked Alexandra Ffoulkes. Guy smiled at her embarrassment.

'Would you like me to carry that bag for you? It looks rather heavy.'

'God bless you, no. It's just my little bit of shopping and we're obviously not going in the same direction. Well, well. Guy Ffoulkes,' she muttered as she went on her way.

Calmer now, the encounter had the

effect of pulling Guy out of what was left of his bad mood, and by the time he reached the Grange he was in a much better frame of mind. *Eight bedrooms, and mine has to be one of the three without en suite.* He smiled at this to-him-unfamiliar austerity. He had the means these days to live in luxury, and he'd be lying if he said he didn't enjoy the trappings of wealth. It was the way it was, unlike in his mother's day when she was at pains to create what she referred to as a good impression. Back then when she had chosen to entertain — which meant getting someone else in to do the work while she acted the gracious hostess — she'd made sure there were adequate facilities. They didn't, however, extend to the whole property. There was no way she was prepared to share her bathroom, but she didn't provide such niceties for her only child. In any case, even if Guy's room had been one of those with an en suite, it would have been given over to one of the residents in his absence.

'How was your walk, Guy?' the manager, Betty Grant, asked as he came in. 'Is Rills Ford as you remembered it?'

'Like a time warp, Betty. I feel as if I must have been whisked here in the Tardis.'

'I think you'll find we've advanced with the years. There's even a free wi-fi connection in Honey's teashop. Did you go to see her? I know how you used to haunt the place.'

It wasn't very subtle, but Betty made the most of the privilege of being an old friend, having been housekeeper in the old days. Family retainers weren't above planning romances any more than the rest of society, and she'd always liked Honey.

Guy's response wasn't quite what she'd hoped for. He brushed off the question by saying, 'Yes, but that was when Basil was there.' He told her he'd walked the length of the High Street, and then quickly changed the subject. 'Would it be all right if we did that inspection now? I'd like to meet the residents. Will I know any of them apart from Daisy Bunting?'

'You'll know them all, Guy. Everyone is local and there's a great demand for places.'

'Hopefully we'll have more space if my plans work out.'

'You're going ahead then?'

Guy had discussed the project with Betty. She would be an integral part of the whole enterprise and he would need her advice and co-operation. It wasn't for her to question his motives in keeping certain aspects secret; he'd asked for her discretion and he would have it.

*   *   *

'How are you, Daisy? I hope you don't mind me using your first name. You never used to when I came into the teashop.'

Guy sat in the chair next to Honey's mother. When he'd entered the room

21

she'd been watching the wall-mounted television, fiddling with the hand control, jumping from one channel to another.

'Now then, my dear, didn't I say we'd put this to one side and leave it on the channel with all your favourite programmes?' Betty said, gently removing the remote from Daisy's fingers. 'Why don't I switch it off for a while and you can have a nice cosy chat with Guy. Do you remember him? He's a friend of Basil's.'

Daisy looked at Guy without any sign of recollection; but when he said, 'I don't know if you recognise me but I certainly remember your chocolate fudge cake,' her face lit up like a beacon.

'It's my favourite too. My children always fight over who's going to lick the bowl. Do you know them?'

'I do indeed; or at least I did. Until this afternoon I hadn't seen Honey for several years.'

'You like honey?'

Guy tried to ignore the renewed feeling of resentment at the mention of her name. 'Of course I do.'

'I prefer jam myself.'

At first he thought she was joking, but then he realised she was a little more confused that he'd first thought. He hoped her memory would mend along with her limbs.

Guy spent a few more minutes with Daisy before going to meet the rest of the residents, all of whom were familiar to him and some of whom were obviously delighted to see him back. After a while he met up with Betty again and told her he was going back into Rills Ford for dinner and not to wait up for him.

★　★　★

It took a lot of resolve for Honey to visit her mother, or at least the Grange, after work. She'd been busy after Guy left and hadn't had time to analyse her feelings. She realised her reaction might

23

have seemed over the top and was ready to discuss Guy's plans with him more calmly — if he was prepared to discuss them at all after the way she'd behaved. *Not that I have any intention of backing down. I meant what I said. Only maybe I was just a bit more forceful than I should have been.*

She needn't have worried. Betty greeted her at the door with the news that Guy had done a tour of inspection and had gone out for dinner. *So much for us eating together.* Honey found her mother watching an old soap.

'Hello, Mum. *Neighbours* again. Does it remind you of Basil?'

'Basil? Is he the one with the long blond hair?'

'No, that's Scott. Basil is your son. He's married now. He lives in Australia with his wife Lucy and their little boy, Tom.'

Honey remembered the photo Guy had given her and took it out of her bag.

'Look, this is Tom; your grandson.'

Daisy looked at the picture with interest. 'See here,' she said, pointing to a cluster of freckles on Tom's cheek and mistaking what they were. 'Naughty boy. I bet he's been at the chocolate bowl, just like his father used to.'

3

At a loose end now that her dinner with Guy hadn't worked out, Honey did what she ought to have been doing in the first place and went home to bake. This was how she usually spent the hours after the shop closed, except on a Saturday, her only regularly free evening. *Just as well he stood me up or I'd have been working half the night. Only he didn't really stand me up, did he? If I'm honest I brought most of it on myself.*

Honey had time to reflect as she was measuring out ingredients. *It's not like me to be on that short a fuse. Was it all about my concern for Mum, or was some of it because Guy threw me off my stride the moment he walked through the door?* She made no attempt to answer that question, but something had certainly upset her because two of her cakes went straight into the bin, an almost unheard-of occurrence. She was satisfied with the rest though, and at nine thirty she phoned Suzie.

'Hello, Suzie. It's Honey. I've just finished baking for the night. I don't suppose you fancy a quick one at the Rose and Crown?'

'I'm sorry, I can't; not a quick one anyway.' Honey heard her giggle. 'I'm already on my second. What do you fancy? A glass of red as usual? I'll have it waiting for you.'

'Just give me five minutes. I've got so much to tell you. You're not going to believe it.'

'Me too.'

Honey walked into the Rose and Crown to find Suzie sitting at the bar talking to Guy of all people. Taking a deep breath, she went to join them. Guy's greeting was polite if somewhat lacking in welcome.

'I hear you two have met already today. Guy's just been telling me about some of his plans for the Grange. I'm

27

thinking of running a small piece in the *Rills Ford Post*. What do you think?

'Guy already knows what I think, though I might have put my reasons a bit too forcefully,' Honey said, smiling at him and hoping this tentative semi-apology would clear the air between them.

'Well I understand your concerns; of course I do. Particularly after I went home and visited all the residents. I thought things were going quite well when I saw Daisy. I mentioned chocolate fudge cake and her eyes lit up, but then she talked about you licking out the bowl and I realised she was thinking about when you were children. Unless you still lick the bowl out,' he replied, meeting her more than halfway.

'I may do occasionally — purely to ensure that I've got the mixture right, you understand. In fact, I've just come from baking another batch.'

'That would account for the chocolate in the corner of your mouth then.'

'You're joking,' she said, absolutely mortified.

'Yep. In fencing I believe it's called a riposte.'

'I can see you haven't lost your somewhat warped sense of humour then. Why don't you pop in tomorrow and sample some of the cakes. It isn't all chocolate fudge.'

'I'd love to. Would the afternoon be okay? I have an appointment at the Planning Department in the morning.'

The atmosphere changed perceptibly as Guy's words reminded her about the project. 'Whenever you like,' Honey replied, but the warmth had gone out of her voice. Soon after that Guy left, and Honey and Suzie moved to a vacant table.

'Fancy him coming back after all this time. Maturity hasn't diminished any of his charm, has it?'

'I'd like to charm him right away from here. And as for maturity . . . chocolate in the corner of my mouth indeed! Don't you see, Suzie? He's come back rich and famous and he thinks he can do the lord of the manor bit.'

'I suppose to some extent he can.'

'Well he can think again. We don't live in a feudal system anymore and I'm not having him ride roughshod over us all just so he can play with his bricks.'

'You think it's that bad?'

'Potentially, Suzie, yes I do. The smallest thing upsets Mum at the moment, though she hides it well. She's hardly even settled in properly yet and you can bet any upheaval will be disturbing. I'm sure some of the others are the same; and this is not the smallest thing by any stretch of the imagination.'

'Yes, but I've been to the Grange and in all honesty I'm not even certain it's fit for use. The heating system is antiquated and some of the doorways have lips; easy to trip over.'

'Whose side are you on?'

'I'm not on anyone's side, but you've got to admit it isn't perfect. I want what's best for the community as much as you do and I appreciate you're closer to it than I am, what with your mum being there. Persuade me if you can that what Guy is proposing is wrong.'

'Right! This may take a while and I need another drink. Same again?'

Honey went to the bar and stood with her back to Suzie while she waited. She spent the time trying to organise her thoughts, to subdue her indignation. When she sat down, armed with a dish of peanuts, she was feeling calmer. Suzie had her notebook open in front of her. If she was going to do an article, Honey knew she would be scrupulously fair and report things as she saw them. Honey would need a strong argument if she wanted to refute the justification of the supposed improvements.

'Guy's very keen, you know, and frank too. He didn't tell me anything I didn't already know about conditions at the Grange. Some of the rooms are en suite but some don't even have a wash basin and toilet. In this day and age that's just not acceptable. One tiny lift was installed when it began functioning as a care home but it's hardly enough in case of emergency. In fact, I'm surprised it's even passed inspection. Convince me why it shouldn't go ahead.'

'Okay, I'll try. For a start let's talk aesthetics. Rills Ford is an old town in the heart of the English countryside. Have you seen any of his work? Do you think a purpose-built structure of that sort would fit in? The expression 'sore thumb' comes to mind. I think the local population would support me on that one, don't you? Secondly, who the hell does he think he is? He's behaving like some Russian oligarch coming in and taking over *our* town. He's dropped out for fourteen years and now he thinks he can waltz right in and take over. Things don't happen like that.'

'I think you might find they do, but carry on; what else?'

'My mum; everybody's mum, and dad, or anyone who might potentially need to go into care. It's homely at the Grange; comfortable; familiar; it's got proper furniture. You know before she went there I looked around to find what would be best for her. Every single place I saw was absolutely soulless. They were clean and tidy but I felt as though I was in a hospital ward.'

'All right, you get a point for that one.'

'It's getting harder, not easier. And if it's not broken, why mend it?'

'But parts of it are broken, Honey. You know that. I need a stronger argument.'

'Many of the elderly are subject to deterioration in their condition if they're stressed, and any change is stressful. Okay, maybe I can see that at the time of initially going into care improved facilities would be beneficial, but for those already there it could be disastrous. Even for the new residents, nobody wants to live in a pseudo-hospital.'

'I agree you've presented your case

well. Give me time to mull it over. Yes, I know you're in a hurry,' Suzie said when she saw impatience spread all over Honey's face, 'but if we're going to have any hope of succeeding we need to think this through carefully. I don't tell you how to do your job so please don't tell me how to do mine.'

'You heard what he said. He's going to the Planning Office tomorrow. We have to do something before he pushes this through.'

4

'You know, Jack, at first I thought she was just being over-emotional about the whole thing, but she does have a point.'

Jack bristled slightly and though Suzie knew he was sweet on Honey, she didn't really think she'd said anything he could take exception to merely because she'd suggested her friend might be a tad carried away by her feelings.

At least he doesn't know how I feel about him. Despite having joined the paper originally because of a schoolgirl crush, I'm a damn fine journalist now and I'd like a bit of credit for what I'm doing.

'You're right; she does.' A couple of years behind Jack in school, Guy had never been one of his favourites, Suzie knew, envying him his easy manner and the way everything had seemingly fallen into his lap. 'I'm not saying he doesn't deserve his success. I'm sure he's a talented man who's worked very hard over the years. But why he wants to come back now and turn the place upside-down beats me,' he said, grudgingly acknowledging the other's achievements.

'Perhaps he genuinely wants his home back. There's plenty of land at the Grange, but it is his land, and he'd be giving it up if he builds a new care home there.'

'And being paid handsomely for the privilege, I have no doubt.'

'You think that's what this is all about, Jack? Money?'

'Why else would a jetsetter come to an out-of-the way place like Rills Ford?'

'Why indeed?'

★ ★ ★

Suzie had had plenty of time overnight to reflect. She could smell a good story a mile off, and this was much closer than that. She had no axe to grind as far as Guy Ffoulkes was concerned, but like most people she wanted to protect her environment. No more than Honey did she want a new care home to be built in the grounds of the Grange, though her reasons weren't entirely the same. Honey's priority, she was sure, was her mother's welfare. The safety of the residents was an important factor to Suzie too, but the prospect of a modern eyesore in her beautiful town weighed heavily on her. Sometime during the night a vague idea had quickly formulated into a definite plan, a plan that would make one helluva good story and with luck would achieve its aims as well.

'I'm thinking of running a piece on Guy, something about him returning to his roots but wanting to plant new pasture,' she said to Jack over a cup of coffee the next morning.

'Okay, we're pretty quiet this week but remember, you've only got until tomorrow evening before we go to press.'

'Leave it to me.'

Suzie knew she'd have to work fast. If Guy was going to the Planning Office this morning, who knew how advanced things were. She had to hope it was only the submission stage. It didn't seem logical that Guy would have put in his application from abroad, and she knew he'd only just returned from Australia. It was more than likely, though, that he'd already completed his architect's drawings. The more she thought about it, the more she felt sure there was time in hand, but not time to waste. She had some planning of her own to do. She drafted her piece and edited it until she was satisfied it was ready to run by Jack.

Famous Rills Ford Boy Returns to his Old Patch

After an absence of fourteen years, renowned architect Guy Ffoulkes returns to put down his roots.

However, in claiming his former home, is he also tearing up those of the current residents? While wishing to restore the Grange to its former glory, Guy plans to create a purpose-built care home within his grounds — but are his intentions admirable or selfish? Do we want a hideous piece of modern architecture within the confines of our town? Whilst I can admire Guy's past creations, everything has its right place, and Rills Ford is not it, not if previous examples of his work are anything to go by.

Secondly, but to no lesser degree, the current occupiers of the Grange are amongst the most vulnerable of our population. For many already sensitive people it might be a turning point ... and not for the better. Will this be the catalyst to send them on the downward spiral? Are we going to stand by and let that happen? How many fortunes does one man need *to make in a lifetime? Your opinions please by email, text or tweet to the usual addresses below.*

★ ★ ★

Suzie took a forty-minute break for lunch and spent it in the Honey Bunny Tearooms. There she found her friend rearranging the various things on offer after the morning coffee customers had made inroads into some of her cakes. There was a small but carefully chosen lunchtime menu which Honey provided not out of choice but as a perceived necessity. Cakes were her speciality, and quiches and fresh sandwiches were bought in from a local though well-thought-of supplier. Morning and afternoon were her busiest times, but there was a steady patronage in the middle of the day for those who wanted either to take something back to their place of work or, more often, sit in the quiet comfort of the tearooms.

'I see you've got that amazing egg and tomato-ey thing again. Perhaps if I just have a small slice I might be able to manage a piece of coffee and walnut gateau.'

'Far be it from me to turn away custom, Suzie, but didn't you say you were trying to cut down?'

'I've spent the morning burning up a lot of calories on my latest story.' She paused for effect. 'The one about Guy.'

Honey sat up and took notice. At least she would have done if she hadn't already been standing. She nearly dropped the quiche on the floor. 'You're running the article then?'

'What do you think? Of course I am. It'll make a great piece. No, don't look at me like that. I'm fully aware of your vested interest but this is important to us all. Glass, steel and sharp lines really don't go hand-in-hand with quaint cottages and thatched roofs. I've decided to organise a petition.'

'That's a fantastic idea!'

'And one to be kept under your hat,

though I agree it's a very pretty hat,' Suzie said, alluding to the white lace mob cap Honey always wore to work. 'It will have much greater impact if it comes out without any foreknowledge. All I have to do now is to try and persuade Jack to run it on the front page.'

After a hastily eaten lunch Suzie went back to the office, more than satisfied with her day so far. She'd sworn Honey to secrecy, trusting that nothing would be said. It wasn't in her friend's interests at all to spike her guns.

He may only have been the proprietor of a provincial newspaper but, like Suzie, Jack knew a good story when he saw one. Suzie was confident he would approve, but she didn't know whether or not something with potentially greater impact would come up that might take precedence. Jack had told her it was a quiet week, but there was still time for something to supersede her article.

'Great work, Suzie. Unless anything else materialises, the front page is yours.'

5

Honey looked up at the sound of the bell expecting at mid-afternoon to see one of her regulars. If she'd had to rely on them totally she'd have been out of business in no time but they were certainly the mainstay, the backbone that kept her afloat. However, it was still a bit early for the tourist season, something she liked to refer to mentally as the icing on the cake. The pun had always made her smile. She managed to hide her astonishment when Guy walked up to the counter. After his comment about visiting the Planning Officer and her somewhat cool response, she hadn't really expected him to turn up this afternoon.

'I went without lunch especially, Honey, and I'm starving.' He tried to look wraith-like but for a man of his stature it was an impossible feat. 'When

I saw what you had here yesterday I knew I'd never be able to choose just one. Do you have any particular recommendations? What shall I begin with?' He was like a kid in a sweet shop.

'Do you want to start off small or go for it straight away?' Honey asked with a smile. She couldn't help responding to Guy's charm and tried to tell herself it was purely business and she a purveyor of delicious irresistible treats. She wasn't fooled for a moment. In spite of her antipathy towards his proposed project, the man had a charisma she knew she would always respond to.

'Impossible to decide.'

'Well, hold on for a minute. I'm just taking Mrs Worthington's scone and tea over. I'll be back to see if I can help.'

'Oh please, let me. I met her in the street yesterday and we had a very quick chat. She's as independent as ever, isn't she? Wouldn't even let me carry her bags. She told me I wasn't going in her direction.'

He smiled as Honey handed the tray over and she wasn't a bit surprised to see him sit down at the old lady's table, the two of them engaging in a conversation she couldn't hear in spite of the fact she tried very hard. *I'm not really being nosy. I just want to make sure my customers are comfortable.* Who did she think she was kidding? In fact it was quite innocuous. The two were reminiscing about the old days and Mrs Worthington was reminding Guy of some of the scrapes he'd got into as a child.

'Do you remember the time when you and Basil Bunting nearly got caught in old Charlie Parker's side garden scrumping his apples?'

'Do I just! If it hadn't been for you opening your bag below hedge level so we could drop them in, we'd have been for it all right.'

'I've never seen him move so quickly. He was out of that gate in a flash, absolutely sure he'd caught you red-handed. He did look suspiciously at my bag, but he could hardly ask me if I had his apples in there.'

'How is the old boy now?'

'He's not with us anymore.'

Guy looked surprised. 'What happened to him? He wasn't that old, was he?'

'Good heavens, no. He's gone to live with his widowed sister up north somewhere. No loss to Rills Ford, I must say. He was a grumpy bugger.'

Guy scraped his chair back. 'I'm sorry, Mrs Worthington. I shall have to leave you now. That scone looks delicious and I can't wait any longer. I'm coming back though to escort you home. No, no arguments. You never know, we may even be able to scrump some apples on the way.'

'Not at this time of the year we won't, but I'm not averse to having a young man keep me company for a while. I'm in no hurry. Take your time.'

Honey wasn't the only one who'd been watching their table with interest. Some of her customers remembered

Guy as a boy, while others, new to the town, wondered who he was. He would always draw attention to himself though, like enticing a moth to a flame. The vicar's wife, Mrs Andrews, had always had a soft spot for him and looked on fondly. He and Bas had often been in trouble, but in a healthy way. Scrumping was about the worst thing they did; *and which of us doesn't do that, given the opportunity?* she wondered.

One or two others were none too pleased to see him back — people who had been offended by his mother; and there were plenty of those, who unfairly tarred Guy with the same brush. Alexandra Ffoulkes had shunned town life and remained in her ivory tower, except when she wanted something, in which case she either made demands or simply opened her purse. In a small community that was not the way to win friends.

Those who didn't know Guy at all just wondered who the stranger was, looking immaculate even in casual clothes. Of course broad shoulders and superb body musculature maintained by regular exercise didn't do him any harm either. An erratic eyebrow and thick brown hair with a wayward quiff at the front added to the whole, and his easy smile had more than once fooled business associates into believing he was a pushover. If he was aware of the attention he was receiving today he certainly didn't show it. Returning to the counter, he found Honey had placed several small samples of deliciousness on a plate in readiness for him.

'I decided as you were having so much difficulty choosing that an assiette would be the answer. Find a table and I'll bring you some tea.'

Honey had expected him to join Mrs Worthington again but he found a place near the window and was gazing out intently when she brought the tray. 'I don't suppose you could join me for a few minutes, could you?'

She looked around. It wasn't very professional, but as none of her customers seemed to need her at the moment she pulled out a chair. 'Just for a moment then.'

Guy glanced out of the window and back again. 'I can't believe how little it's changed. I'd almost forgotten places like this existed.'

Honey was about to protest at what she perceived as criticism when he continued. 'It's amazing. I'm so glad I've come home.'

She chose not to rise to the bait, if bait it was. Now wasn't the time raise the matter and she didn't want to have a disagreement with him every time they met. In any case, he was talking about the town, not his project at the Grange. Instead she changed the subject.

'So what do you think? Any particular favourite?'

'It's a close-run thing, and of course I haven't sampled the scones yet.'

'It can be arranged.'

The laugh reached his eyes and he clutched his stomach theatrically. 'Another time, Honey, another time. It is imperative they are accompanied by jam and cream, lots of cream. I fear that for today, at least, I have had my fill.'

'I'm always here if you want to come back again.' Honey hoped she hadn't spoken too eagerly.

'Don't worry, I shall. I've been thinking. I might have a small business proposition for you.'

Oh no. Not something else for me to get upset about. Honey had no time to respond as the doorbell rang and she returned to the counter to serve her next customer. By the time she'd finished, Guy and Mrs Worthington were on their feet and preparing to leave. Guy came over to pay the bills; he'd insisted on paying for Mrs Worthington as well, and Honey wasn't sure whether or not she approved. She decided she was being silly. He wasn't throwing his money around; he was merely being polite. And if the old lady didn't object, why should she?

'About that proposition, Honey — any chance we could have a chat up at the Grange after you've seen your mother?'

'If it won't take too long, yes of course we can. I have to get back to do some baking though; replenish my depleted stock now that you've been here.' She tried a wry smile that she didn't quite manage to pull off.

'Be sure to make some scones. I'll be back tomorrow for some of those.'

'Some?' she couldn't resist asking.

'One would be teasing, but if I'm to make this a regular occurrence I'd better find a gym.'

She wasn't sure if he was teasing or serious.

★   ★   ★

Honey had some colour photos which she'd cut into several pieces to show Daisy. One was of herself as a child, one a picture of the facade of Honey Bunny

Tearooms, and the third a magnificent chocolate gateau.

'What do you think of these, Mum?'

She placed the one of the shop in front of her mother on the small table and helped her piece it together. Daisy, using her good hand to support the one with the fractured wrist, smiled as she put in the last cut-out, and a huge smile lit up her face when she saw the completed picture.

'Chocolate fudge cake! My favourite.'

Honey picked up the bits of paper and replaced them with the others, suggesting that Daisy try to do the puzzle alone this time. Again she used one hand to help the other and again she completed the picture. Honey was delighted. It was the first time she'd tried this and she hadn't been confident of its success, but her determined mother wasn't going to let the inconvenience of a useless wrist stand in her way. She felt encouraged to experiment further another time and resolved to speak to Betty Grant to see if she had any suggestions.

It was time for Daisy's favourite soap and Honey switched on the television. Her mother seemed to be able to forget about the pain — of which she never complained — when losing herself in its familiar characters and situations. Honey left her to it and went to find Guy. She didn't have far to go. He was hovering outside, waiting for her.

'You should have come in. I'm sure she'd have liked to see you.'

'I spent a while with her earlier. I didn't want to intrude on your time together.'

'How was she? Earlier I mean.'

'A little mixed-up maybe, but only for a moment and nothing much to speak of.'

'Yes, I've noticed them too — those moments — but I'm sure they're less frequent than before. The doctors said they hoped it would pass in time and it looks like they were right.'

'So, are you up for that discussion?'

'Discussion, is it? That sounds

important. Can we go into the garden? It's a lovely evening and there's a large patio area where we sometimes sit with our relatives when the weather's nice, but of course you know that.'

'The garden it is. Would you like some tea?'

'No, thank you. I'm fine. In any case I didn't bring any cake with me.'

'Just as well after the amount I had this afternoon. That's what I wanted to talk to you about actually,' he said as they sat in the cool of the evening sun.

'How much cake you had! Don't you go blaming me if you've got tummy-ache.'

'No, of course not. This is a business proposition. I noticed most of your cakes were gateaux. There weren't many individual pastries.'

'It's the character of the place,' she interrupted, feeling attacked.

'For goodness sake, stop being so prickly and let me finish, Honey.'

Am I prickly? I suppose I am. Only since you came back though.

'Would you be prepared to provide mini-patisserie to the Grange, say twice a week? The food here is excellent, but I think it would be nice if the residents could have something special occasionally. Not every day, because then it wouldn't mean the same thing. Maybe on Sundays and perhaps Wednesdays as a special treat.' He was quite excited. She could see it. 'We could arrange them on trays so people could pick their own, though I rather fancy your mother's would always be chocolate fudge.' They both smiled at the thought. 'And we'd have to be careful they didn't dip their fingers first into one and then another. I just thought it would make it a bit special if they could choose for themselves.'

'It's a lovely idea, Guy.'

'Yes, that's what I thought. That's why I'm suggesting little pastries instead of big cakes. Is it something you could do? Time-wise, I mean. Can you fit it into your schedule? I know less than nothing about baking, but even I realise it's a lot more work making lots of little things than one big one.'

'The mixture will be the same. It just means dividing them into pastry cases instead of a cake tin. Of course the decorating will take longer, but I love doing it.'

'And if you do the tiny ones maybe they could have two.'

'And you're going to grow up when, exactly?'

'Never, I hope.'

'Would you like me to give you an estimate?'

'Certainly not. It will be my little contribution.'

Honey had absolutely no idea about Guy's other 'little' contributions and he wasn't about to tell her. He couldn't resist taking credit for this one though. They parted amicably this time and Honey went home to plan, grateful for the prospect of added income even though it would take up much more of her precious time.

6

Next day what began as a hum became the talk of the town by lunchtime. Suzie's article appeared, on the front page as Jack had promised, and its impact was huge. Through no fault of his own Guy had unfortunately inherited his mother's reputation. It was unfair and unreasonable but there were mutterings like 'The apple doesn't fall far from the tree' and 'She always thought she owned this place and now he's trying to do the same'. Several copies of the *Rills Ford Post* were delivered every week to the Grange for those residents who wanted to enjoy the local news, so it wasn't long before Guy became aware of what felt like a hate campaign against him. To say he was stunned would be to underestimate the wounded feelings that seemed to permeate every part of his body. There was a constriction in his throat that made him feel he was choking until anger raised its head above all other emotions.

Why are they attacking me like this? They don't even know me.

Guy had been more than enthusiastic when he'd spoken to Suzie about his plans. He'd realised pretty quickly from Honey's reactions that it wasn't going to go down well universally, but Suzie had given him no idea she felt so strongly against the project. The fact that she hadn't raised any objections at the time and had now turned on him with such vitriol only accentuated his feeling of betrayal.

She's a journalist out for a good story. I don't blame her for that. It's her job.

Understanding the reasons didn't in any way excuse them in Guy's mind. He didn't remember much about Suzie from their younger days, so he had no idea if her apparent ruthlessness was a character trait or learned behaviour.

Either way, he wasn't taking it lying down and he decided to confront her on her own territory. So anxious was he to have it out with her that he took his rather swish car into the town, the first time in the few days he'd been home that he'd used it. He rather liked that everything was within walking distance and his outings so far were reacquainting him with his past, especially his childhood. He'd completely forgotten about the scrumping incident until Mrs Worthington had reminded him, and he realised there were a lot of things he'd consigned to a closed box somewhere in the recesses of his mind. The lid had come off now and long-hidden memories were flooding in.

As he drove down the main street he saw Honey putting a couple of bistro tables and chairs outside the tearooms. Spring was in the air, in spite of a definite chill, and sitting watching the world go by was a rather appealing prospect he didn't have time for right now.

She works so hard. I wonder what would have happened to her if circumstances had been different.

Among Guy's other memories was the one when he'd received a threat from Basil. They were sixteen at the time and filled with testosterone. Guy was unconscious of his looks and his natural charm — his mother had eradicated any self-confidence he might have had — and his pursuit of the young female population was more in hope than expectation. In spite of his success in that area he'd never been able to believe it was due to anything other than the fact that he lived in 'the big house'. As he became successful in business this was reinforced when every girlfriend had made him feel like a trophy. His reputation as a womaniser had been inflicted on him as he rejected one after another, and he'd hidden behind its protection.

In all his life only one girl had stood apart from the rest, accepted him for who he was, and that one girl had always treated him as a friend, never giving any indication she'd like to be more. *And not much has changed since then*, he thought, remembering Basil's warning. 'If you lay a finger on my sister it will be the last thing you ever do.' Since he was convinced any approach from him would have been unwelcome, Basil's words were unnecessary. When he'd kissed the top of her head on his departure to university she'd shrugged him aside. What more proof was needed? And now, when he would love to have included her in his plans, he found she was completely against the whole concept, condemning it without ever knowing the details. *Which brings me nicely to Suzie Foster*, he thought, as he parked outside the offices of the *Rills Ford Post*.

* * *

'Come in, Guy. It's good to see you,' Jack said, extending his hand in greeting. 'It's been a long time. Nice to see you've done well for yourself.'

Guy had no option but to take the proffered hand as he was drawn into the building. 'It's great to be back, Jack, but . . . ' He left the sentence hanging in the air.

'I expect you'd like to talk to Suzie. She's through here.' Jack led Guy to a small windowless office at the back where Suzie sat, not looking a bit like someone bent on another's destruction. 'I'll leave you together.'

'Why, Suzie? What have I ever done to you?' he asked as he took the seat she gestured to.

'Nothing, Guy. You know that. But surely you can see how this affects everyone. I know you've been away for a long time, but you can't have forgotten what it's like here; how much pride everyone takes in their surroundings.'

'No, of course I haven't, but that doesn't explain a full frontal attack. You didn't give me any indication when we met the other night that you felt so strongly. In fact, you were encouraging me to talk about it.'

Suzie couldn't help smiling.

'Yes, I know you're a reporter and any potential story needs to be pounced upon, but this was something different. You didn't ask me about design. You didn't ask to see the plans. Whatever makes you think I'm not amongst the rest who take pride in their neighbourhood? You've condemned me out of hand and you've done it publicly.' Guy didn't raise his voice but it had a steely edge to it.

'It's my job, Guy.'

'No doubt, but was this the only way you could go about it?'

'If you must know, it seemed the best way to get support quickly. Your plans haven't been passed yet and I'm going to do everything I can to make sure they're not. The last thing we want is a blot on our beautiful landscape.'

'I'm sure you'll get a lot of support from your readers. You've appealed to their basic emotions with your very one-sided article. I just wanted to let you know I'm not going away. I believe in this project and I'm going to see it through. In case you're wondering why I've come here, it's to let you know I don't do things underhandedly. You've crossed the wrong person this time, Suzie.'

*　*　*

In spite of his cool appearance Guy was so wound up he thought better of taking the car and decided to walk off his rage. No doubt about it, Rills Ford was picturesque. Leaving the main road, Guy wove his way through the long-forgotten but vaguely familiar roads. Each house was different to its neighbour, varying in size and appearance, but every one was worthy of the epithet 'chocolate-box cottage'. He knew that in a couple of months there would be a profusion of colour as wisteria, clematis and honeysuckle flowers adorned walls that at present seemed as if they were covered in dead wood.

Honeysuckle. Seems I just can't get away from her.

He passed the tiny dwelling that was home to Mrs Worthington and hesitated, thinking he might pay her a visit. No, he wasn't quite ready for people yet. Another turn brought him to the town school where children were running around in the playground. Guy looked at his watch. The *Rills Ford Post* hadn't arrived at the Grange until mid-morning and though he'd gone straight to see Suzie, he'd been walking for a while now. His watch told him it was lunchtime and explained why the playground was full. He paused at the gates, old memories flooding back, and was surprised when a voice from the other side said, 'Guy? How lovely to see you. I'd heard you were back.'

Guy found himself staring into the face of Mary Simpson, his old teacher, and was a child again. In those days primary teachers went right through the school with their pupils, and Mary Simpson had been one of the few people who'd recognised Guy's loneliness and knew the reason for it.

'Mrs Simpson! You're still here!'

'I'm not that old, Guy, though it must seem that way to you. I'm headmistress now.'

'I didn't mean to be rude. It was just all such a long time ago.'

'And you went away, made your fortune and now you're back again,' she said, but kindly. 'I always knew you were destined for great things.'

Guy tried to hide his embarrassment. 'Not great.'

'You were always a good student. You tried so hard to please. I expect that was compensation for what you were going through at home.'

'You knew.'

'Of course I knew, and from what I've seen in today's paper you're still carrying the burden of your mother with you today.'

'You've seen it then.'

'There will be few who haven't. A small place like this likes its local news. Don't be too hard on Suzie.' *How does she know?* 'She's only doing her job, and doing it well, even if you don't like the circumstances. It's up to you to put your own side of the story. I'm sure you have one.'

Suddenly Guy didn't seem quite so alone. 'I do, but it isn't one I want made public at the moment. Mrs Simpson, I could hug you.'

'It's just as well we're on opposite sides of this gate then. Whatever would the children think?'

'I wonder, would it be an imposition if I came to see you from time to time? There are things I'd like to talk about and I trust you to honour a confidence.'

'The school phone number's up there on the board. Make a note of it. Calls are diverted to me when there's no one here. I'd love to see you, and you're right — anything you tell me will remain between the two of us.'

Mary Simpson had always been an

ally, and it seemed that hadn't changed. Guy walked on feeling a whole lot better.

★ ★ ★

Suzie, on the other hand, wasn't feeling better. She was feeling guilty. *Did I jump the gun? Was I really that unfair?* 'What do you think, Jack? Was I too quick off the mark?'

Jack saw a vulnerability in Suzie he hadn't known was there. She'd always presented such a go-getting image, he'd assumed she was as self-assured as she appeared. Obviously that wasn't the case, and the 'new' Suzie had a certain amount of appeal. Suddenly he felt protective towards her.

'It's a good story, Suzie, and I wouldn't have given you the front page if it didn't deserve it.'

Suzie told him what Guy had said, that she'd never seen the plans.

'And what difference would that make? We've all seen examples of his work. In any case, even though the Grange is private property, it's part of this place as much as every other individual building that lines our roads. Whatever he chooses to build would also be part of it. Somehow, to my mind at least, a custom-built care home would stick out like a sore thumb. Why couldn't he just leave it as it is?'

'He wanted to come home.'

'He should have thought of that before he leased the Grange for its current use.'

In all honesty Suzie could see Guy's dilemma. If he wanted to return to his roots, why shouldn't he? Rills Ford was like that. It became a part of you. Why shouldn't he reclaim his heritage? It was the proposed new building she had a problem with.

7

Honey was pretty busy in the tearooms. When she wasn't serving she was attempting to balance her books and figure out a costing for the patisserie Guy had asked her about. She always tried to do her admin stuff during quiet times at work, as most of her evenings were spent in the kitchen — something that would increase if she took up Guy's offer. At this time of year she was almost into her savings — the meagre ones she had — hanging on by her fingertips until the tourist season began. The extra income would be very welcome and she was excited about having an opportunity to expand her artistic talents.

Consequently, it wasn't until mid-afternoon that she even glanced at her own copy of the *Rills Ford Post*. As soon as she saw the headline she sat down to have a proper look, keeping an eye on her customers in case they needed her.

Oh my God, Suzie, that really is hitting hard!

Honey had reservations as to whether or not Suzie had overstepped the mark, but she was no journalist and it was certainly an eye-catching headline, followed by a piece that packed a huge punch. There was also a rather nice photo of Guy. Honey wondered where Suzie had got it from. She also wondered for a moment if Guy had seen it yet — the article not the photo — and what he thought.

I can't worry about that though. It may be a bit strong, but if it stops the development and helps my mother and the rest of them that's all I care about.

In truth she cared about a lot more. For one thing, she was certain Guy wasn't on the make. It didn't fit his character. For another, although she'd convinced herself she'd left her feelings for him behind years ago, she was honest enough to acknowledge to herself it wasn't true. Not that she would ever tell a soul. Not even Suzie. Suzie had never known how Honey felt about Guy. Nobody had, and that was the way she was going to keep it.

Oddly enough, none of her customers seemed to have seen the paper because, as usual for her afternoon cup of tea, Mrs Worthington asked Honey if she could have a look when she'd finished.

'I was that busy this morning I didn't get a chance to read my own copy. Good gracious, if I'd seen this I'd have made sure I did,' she said when Honey handed it to her. 'Mine was folded over with the banner side down so I didn't see the headline. Look, you can see it's just into the top half of the page.'

Once she'd read it everyone else wanted to as well. With the exception of Mrs Worthington, perhaps the only person in Rills Ford apart from Mary Simpson who sensed what Guy was really like, they were unanimous in their condemnation of the proposal.

'Just like his mother, he is, and I never liked her either,' one said.

'She cut me dead every time she saw me. I wasn't good enough for the likes of her,' said another.

There was more, a lot more, and it became a hate campaign against Alexandra Ffoulkes, rather than a consideration of the impact the changes might have on Rills Ford.

Honey didn't join in the conversation. She was keeping a low profile until she had more information. Whatever she might think of Guy's plans, this wasn't about his mother. It was about hers. A sudden hush descended on the tearooms as the man himself walked in.

'Good afternoon, ladies,' he said affably. 'I hope you're all well.'

If he noticed the strained atmosphere he gave no indication of having done so. Guy was no fool. Even without a copy of the *Rills Ford Post* lying on one of the tables, he would have to have been completely insensitive not to be aware of an unsettling silence. Unsettling to the ladies, that was. He was completely at ease. Having left Mary Simpson at the school, he'd collected his car and driven the short distance to a small patch of woodland with the river that gave the town its name running through it. Already wearing casual clothes, he took his walking shoes from the boot of the ear and spent a peaceful couple of hours renewing his acquaintance with one of his favourite childhood haunts. He chose not to step on the boulders across the gently flowing water. As a boy he'd got his feet wet more than once, but he didn't have spare socks with him, and adulthood had brought with it at least a small semblance of common sense. That's not to say he wasn't tempted.

By the time he walked into the Honey Bunny Tearooms he was ravenous! 'I'm looking to you to save my life, Honey. Please tell me you have some sandwiches left from lunchtime or, better still, quiche and salad. I'm not used to all this fresh air and it's given me an appetite.'

'Quiche I can do. Hot or cold?'

'Hot, please.'

'What fresh air? I saw your car go past before,' she said, sorry immediately that she'd mentioned it in case he thought she was looking out for him.

'I've been walking in the woods; you know, like we used to when we were kids.'

'And you used to push me off my balance into the water. Yes, I remember. How did you say you wanted that quiche? Over your head, was it?' she said, taking it out of the microwave and putting it on a tray with a bowl of salad. 'Anything to drink with this?'

'A pot of tea with your little honey bee on the outside would be lovely.'

'Coming right up.'

Honey knew most of the people in the café were giving her sideways glances, and they weren't complimentary either, but this was her place and she owed it to every customer to give the best service she could. Anyway, she didn't like that she could see this becoming a vendetta against Guy rather than a protest about his project.

'Won't you join an old lady, Guy? That is if you don't mind watching me eat cake. I can recommend it when you've finished your lunch.'

At least one of them's on his side

'My pleasure, Mrs Worthington. It's always lovely to sit and chat with you.'

Mrs Worthington was delighted too. Even at her age she wasn't immune to Guy's charm. Knowing he had a sense of humour, she made the most of the situation that had fallen into her lap. 'Have you seen this, Guy?' she said, pointing to the paper. 'It seems there are those who don't approve of what you're trying to do. What do you have to say for yourself?'

Guy was delighted. He knew she was an ally. 'I'm trying to do what's best for Rills Ford and, more particularly, for those in my care. And it would be nice too to have my old home back,' he added mischievously.

'In your care? You've been away all this time and you say these people are in your care?'

'The assumption is that because I've not been here there hasn't been any contact. It would be better all round if assumptions weren't made and conclusions reached without possession of all the facts.' He threw a quick glance at Honey, hoping he'd made his point.

'Well, we all know how people love to gossip. Making mountains out of molehills, that's what they're doing.'

Guy silently blessed the old lady. He might almost have been feeding her the lines; everything she said was designed to make a point. No fool, Mrs Worthington. Guy made an on-the-spot decision and hoped he wouldn't regret it later. 'How about coming up to the Grange tomorrow and having tea with me? The catering is excellent and I could discuss my plans with you if you like.'

Mrs Worthington beamed at him. She knew she was being drawn into a conspiracy but she didn't care. If the whole of the town was conspiring against Guy, he deserved to have one or two people on his side. Apart from which, it was the most exciting thing that had happened to her in years.

'I've got a few old friends living there. It's a while since I've seen them. Yes, Guy, I'd be delighted. I'll visit them first and then we can have a nice little coze.'

Honey had watched this exchange from behind the counter. Everybody in the place had watched, though a few at least kept up some pretence of having their afternoon tea. *What's he up to now?* she wondered.

'That was delicious, Honey, thank you. Now, what about one of your lovely scones? I've been wanting to try them ever since I saw Mrs Worthington eat one with so much enthusiasm the other day. Do you have any raspberry jam? I prefer it to strawberry.'

Honey couldn't help chuckling to herself, though she maintained a business-like exterior. He was working them all just like the professional he was. She wasn't surprised he was so successful in his work. He could charm an angry bull.

'Raspberry jam it is.'

Only human, Honey found herself wondering about Guy's invitation to Mrs Worthington. He was up to something, she was sure of that, and it wouldn't be taking advantage of an old lady. He was a nice guy. *I remember the first time I heard that. I must have been about six and I thought they were talking about him. I stroked his arm and said, 'Nice Guy; nice Guy'. Oh my God, how embarrassing. I hope he doesn't remember.* Honey could only speculate, but for the first time ever she was feeling tied to the premises. It was Saturday the next day but she wouldn't be able to go and see Daisy until early evening, by which time the afternoon tête-à-tête would be well and truly over.

During the summer she always hired a student to help her in the shop. Maybe the extra income from the patisserie would enable her to do that at Easter as well. She could bake during the day and at least have a couple of evenings free for socialising. *I need to get a life!* Only it had never bothered her before. She had to ask herself who she might be wanting to see on those evenings off — as if she didn't know already.

I'm still his best friend's kid sister. In his eyes I'll never be anything else. In any case, she thought, *the sparks are going to fly over this petition. Nobody is going to ride roughshod through my mother's life.*

Honey felt better after her inward rant. She'd been more than content with her single life. That wasn't going to change just because her knight in shining armour had returned from the crusades. He wasn't here to rescue her and she certainly was no damsel in distress. She wondered what the chances were of pumping Mrs Worthington when she came in again on Monday. Probably not great.

8

When Guy got home he phoned Mary Simpson.

'Hello, Guy. How lovely to hear from you again so soon.'

'I was wondering, Mrs Simpson, if you were free to come for tea tomorrow afternoon. I'd like to ask your advice.'

'I'd be more than delighted to help if I can. You don't have to offer me tea as well, young man.'

'Mrs Worthington is coming too. What more could a man ask than to have his two favourite ladies share his table?'

'You've lost none of your charm over the years, Guy Ffoulkes, have you? Will three o'clock suit you?'

'I'll look forward to it.'

Guy took a deep breath. *I wonder if I'm doing the right thing. Only time will tell.*

* * *

Come Saturday morning, Guy couldn't resist going into Honey's tearooms to buy some pastries. The catering up at the Grange would have been more than adequate but somehow he was drawn to the little shop in the main street. Basil's warning to him all those years ago still had the power to pull him up short. Apart from that, in spite of Honey's polite exterior, she'd made it perfectly clear that she didn't approve of him — and it wasn't just his plans for the Grange. He wondered how much was due to his friend's feedback over the years. Guy had made some foolish errors in the romance stakes, going from one girl to another, always ending any relationship before they might think there was a future in it. His heart had long ago been lost to a tomboy — though he had to admit she was no tomboy these days — and he had inadvertently built himself a reputation as a womaniser. He was as certain as he could be that Basil would have kept his sister informed of his friend's progress over the years, not through any malice but because they'd all been so close as children. So what was he doing walking into the shop — again? *I'm buying cakes; that's what I'm doing.*

'Good morning, Honey. I've come to buy some of your delicious cakes. I have visitors for tea this afternoon,' he said, his eyes laughing at her because they both knew that she knew that he knew ... well, that she'd heard the arrangements being made.

'Would you like anything special, or shall I choose for you?'

'Everything is special, Honey. Yes, please choose for, say, six. Just in case I fancy something later on.'

Guy would have been reassured had he known how much his visits upset her composure.

'Of course, the mini ones would have been nicer if you have guests,' she said as she handed him a box of assorted slices of gateaux. 'I've been working on my quote. I'll get it to you tomorrow if that's okay.'

'Talking about tomorrow, am I right in thinking you close on Sundays?'

'Fortunately I do, except in the summer when I have some help. I tried opening seven days a week, and goodness knows I need the income, but there's only so much one person can do. What with spending so much time in the kitchen as well, I have to have some time off.' *Now why did I have to tell him the story of my life?*

'Fancy a walk down by the river? I couldn't help thinking when I was there yesterday how much we all used to enjoy it.'

'What?'

'A walk. By the river. It's what people do. I promise not to push you off the boulders if that's any incentive.'

'It would be more of an incentive if I could push you off. However, comparing your size and mine and remembering what a toad you were, I think I'd come off worse in that encounter. Yes, a walk would be lovely. Thank you.'

'Toads! We could look for toads.'

'You're such a child.'

★   ★   ★

'Make yourself comfortable, ladies. I'll just go and organise some refreshments.'

Guy came back a few minutes later followed by Betty Grant, who was wielding a trolley laden with dainty sandwiches and some of Honey's delicious cakes. She set them on the table and was turning to leave when Guy said, 'No, please don't go. I'd like you to join us if you wouldn't mind.' She looked at her watch. 'Unless you have something urgent,' he said, noticing the gesture.

'I'll just pop off for a couple of minutes to arrange for someone else to do the residents' tea. I usually incorporate it with my afternoon rounds, but I can do that later. I won't be long.

Please start without me, but you be sure to save one of those pastries.'

'You'd better be quick. They may not last that long,' Guy said, smiling as she scuttled out.

Mary insisted on pouring the tea, by which time Betty had returned.

'You may all be wondering why I've asked you here today — not that it isn't a pleasure to entertain you any time, but there's obviously more to it than that on this occasion.'

'And there we were thinking you just wanted to reminisce about old times,' said Mrs Worthington with something remarkably resembling a twinkle in her eye.

'Yes, while you were out organising tea Dorothy was just telling me about the apple episode, and asking what kind of mischief you used to get up to in school. I told her you were a model pupil.'

'I knew I could rely on your discretion, which brings me nicely to the point. I'm laying my trust in you all, not because I want you to spy for me — I wouldn't dream of asking you that.' He paused, his eyes as alight with laughter as Mrs Worthington's, knowing full well there wasn't very much happening in Rills Ford that these three women didn't know about.

'It's about your plans for the Grange?' said Mary.

'Yes. Betty here knows exactly what I have in mind, and I'm hoping it will serve several ends, but at the moment I'm being tarred by the brush of my mother's reputation.'

All three women watched him sympathetically: Betty, because she'd been housekeeper at the Grange in Alexandra's day; Mary, because as his teacher she knew how cold the young boy's family had been and how much it had dented his confidence and self-esteem; and Dorothy, because she had been his and Basil's youthful guardian angel. Scrumping wasn't the only scrape she'd got them out of. He'd chosen his allies well.

Guy stood and went over to a large dresser to retrieve some rolled-up papers. 'When we've finished our tea I'd like you to have a look at these. I think you might find them interesting. Betty's seen them already, of course. Any plans for the care home had to have her approval first, in my opinion. But there's more.'

'Let's have a look now,' said Mrs Worthington. 'I've always taken my tea cold.'

'Well I haven't. When you're a teacher you have to throw it back while it's still scalding or the bell is calling you away before you've had a chance to drink it. As headmistress it's a bit more civilised, but I've never lost the habit.'

'There's no hurry. Maybe you'd like to tell us what happened at the Honey Bun. Guy said there was quite a reaction to Suzie's article.'

'There certainly was, Betty, and I must say this young man handled it beautifully.'

They continued to talk about the

townspeople's comments until they'd finished their tea, Betty pointing out that the sins of the mother were being visited on the child.

A set of plans and elevations were laid on the table, held down by anything that could be used as a paperweight.

'There are plans for the Grange as well, but it's all internal work and needn't concern you. What I'd really like is your opinion on these, but it may be helpful if I give you a bit of background information first.'

'I can hear a bell frantically ringing, Guy. Do you mind if I just go and check? It may be nothing, but I don't like my charges to get agitated.'

'Of course, Betty. There isn't anything here you don't know about, but please come back if you have the chance. Why don't we sit down while we're waiting,' he said to the other two, 'and I'll fill you in.'

'That girl can certainly bake,' Mrs Worthington said, cutting one of the remaining pieces of cake in half. 'I shouldn't, I know, but they're irresistible. So come on, Guy, what is all this really about?'

'Some of it you already know. It's in the public domain. There are other things, things I don't want spread about, and as such I'm putting my faith in three of the four women who acted *in loco parentis* when my mother had better things to do. Daisy, of course, can't help, but she's as much involved as anyone and more than most. The Grange has been her home for some time, and I know Honey is concerned about the effect any change would have on her and the other residents.'

'I believe change isn't good for people as they get older,' Mary responded. 'Familiarity is very important.'

'It's something I'm well aware of. What Honey doesn't know — what nobody knows apart from Betty — is that the facilities here are inadequate for the job we're trying to do. It's only because of the proposed plan that we've been allowed to continue functioning. The Grange isn't fit for use, but we are being given a stay of execution until such time as the residents can be rehoused.'

'Why haven't you told anyone? It would have got you off the hook straight away.'

'You saw what happened at the Honey Bun, Dorothy. What chance have I been given to explain? Exactly,' he said when there was no reply. 'Ah, Betty, glad you could make it back. I was just telling Dorothy and Mary about how we're hanging on by our fingertips.'

'That's a relief. I must admit I didn't like carrying the responsibility alone.'

'Nor should you. The responsibility is mine, and so must the solution be. There are two options as I see it. We could gut this place and bring it up to an acceptable standard — but where would the residents go while all that was going on? Or we could have something purpose-built where every thought has gone into making it as right as possible for anyone who lives there.'

Guy had their interest, he could see that. No one spoke, so he continued.

'This is no sudden whim. It's been on my mind for some time to come home, and obviously I've been in constant contact with Betty here. I drew up the plans a while ago. Maybe you'd like to look at them now.'

They moved to the table where Dorothy and Mary had their first look at Guy's vision for the future, but futuristic it was not. The elevation of the proposed care home showed its architecture to be in the same style as the Grange itself, not the modern monstrosity people had jumped to the wrong conclusion about. The plan showed the internal places to be divided into living quarters, each with its own bathroom, several reception rooms, a state-of-the-art kitchen and dining room, a small hairdressing salon, and three other spaces which as yet had no designation.

'It's magnificent, Guy. But . . . '

'Wait a moment if you will, Mary. Before you say anything I'd like you to see the rest.' He moved back to the dresser and pulled out another set of plans which he laid on top of the first. 'This is a second project which at the moment nobody in Rills Ford seems to know about, though they're at perfect liberty to go to the Planning Office and see what's been lodged.'

'A block of flats!'

'Yes, Dorothy, but not any block of flats. You can see the same architectural design in the elevation here and the fact that there are only two storeys. The idea is that this building, too, will stand in the grounds. Let's face it, there's a huge acreage here which nobody has an opportunity to appreciate. Of course now that I'm home, I could spend my days walking my 'territory', but I'd much sooner see it being put to good use.'

'But why would you want people living on your property, Guy?' asked Mary.

'These flats — as you can see, there are only eight — are intended for staff and family members of the home's residents. While most of the people are local, some of their relatives are not. Two of the flats will be left for the use of those visiting relatives, thus encouraging them to come while at the same time enhancing the quality of life of our own people.'

Dorothy and Mary were beginning to get a glimpse of a suspected-but-before-unseen side of Guy Ffoulkes.

'You're talking huge investment here, Guy. How do you propose to finance such a large project?'

'It's a good question, Mary, and that's where the confidentiality part comes in. Shall we sit down again, and I'll explain.'

Once they were all settled Guy took his time, looking from one to the other to reassure himself he was doing the right thing. He saw only trust and trustworthiness.

'I intend to finance it myself.'

'What?'

'It will cost a fortune. Two fortunes.'

'Yes, Dorothy, I know, but I'm a very rich man. I've been lucky enough to reach a level of wealth where the money comes in much faster than it goes out. What I'm about to tell you now must go no further than this room.'

The ladies looked hurt, as if disappointed he thought they might betray his confidence.

'No, don't look like that. It wasn't an accusation, it was a statement. I have several projects like this one all over the world. I will provide the finance and the land to build. After that the two buildings will be run as a single non-profit concern. Fees will necessarily have to be charged, but they will only be at a level to cover costs, and a trust will be set up to administer the whole. I absolutely do not want the local population to be aware of my role in this. Most people have condemned me, and that's up to them. Far be it from me to shatter their illusions.'

Alexandra Ffoulkes has a lot to answer for, Mary thought. *He isn't going to court anyone's affection in case it's thrown back in his face.*

'It shall be as you wish,' she said. 'Why have you told us?'

Guy smiled and they all saw the vulnerable boy again. 'I'm not immune. I wanted to have some friends on my side. That, and the fact that there's nothing that goes on in this place without one or the other of you knowing about it.'

9

As luck would have it, Sunday dawned bright and beautiful, the sky showing that deep blue that only occurs in autumn and spring. Honey couldn't help feeling a frisson of anticipation as she showered and dressed. She packed a picnic hamper in the hope the weather would keep its promise, and was ready and waiting when Guy arrived at ten o'clock as arranged.

'My goodness, this takes me back,' he said when he saw her in colourfully striped woolly gloves and a hat that couldn't quite control her escaping curls. 'You look like a child again.'

'I feel like one.'

'What's that?' Guy asked, pointing to the backpack as she worked her arms into its straps.

'Picnic. Oh, are you in a hurry? I didn't think.'

'No, I've got all day. Here, give it to me. A picnic is a lovely idea. I've got a rug in the car, but there were plenty of available tree stumps when I went there the other day.'

'You're taking the car?'

'Only so we can make the most of our time there.'

'I can't get into your beautiful car with walking boots on.'

'Of course you can. They're dry, aren't they? Look, if it'll make you feel better take another pair with you just in case.'

'In case you push me into the river,' she said, smiling but challenging.

'I promised I wouldn't do that, and I never break a promise.'

Honey knew this to be the truth from things Basil had let drop when they were children. She was quite sure it had led to Guy taking the rap for someone else on more than one occasion. Not Basil — he would never have allowed that to happen — but there were others who were less principled.

* * *

'It's just as I remember it. Like you, Guy, I haven't been here for years. What a beautiful day you've picked. You might have ordered it.'

'Who's to say I didn't?'

'You may be very tall, but I don't think that's what's meant by being nearer to God.'

After a wrangle over who would carry the backpack — a wrangle which Honey lost, because arguing was silly even if her independent spirit found it difficult to give in — they moved at a steady pace into the woods and joined the river bank, following the water upstream. Neither spoke for some time. There was no awkwardness between them; each was enjoying the peace of the day and the companionable silence.

After a while Honey stopped. Three paces ahead before he realised, Guy turned round with a raised eyebrow, concern written clearly on his face. Honey's stomach did a somersault. It was a look just like the one that had caused her to lose her heart to him all those years ago. She'd tripped and grazed her knees and he'd helped her up. Characteristically she'd brushed him off, assuring him she was okay. He'd shrugged then and moved on. They were twelve and fourteen at the time.

'Is something wrong?' he asked her now.

'Coffee. I need coffee.' She smiled up into his face and he smiled back, but turned away almost immediately. She couldn't have known how much he wanted to take her in his arms.

'Ah, your table awaits, madame,' he said, leading her to a fallen trunk where someone before them had smoothed away the bark to make a suitable resting place. This early in the year the trees weren't in full leaf yet, only the buds promising what was to come. The sun shone through the branches, dappling the ground beneath.

'I remember Bas and I used to come

fishing here. We rarely caught anything, but if we did we always threw it back. Nobody ever believed us when we said we'd hooked one that was this big,' he said, stretching his arms out as far as they would reach, the sparkle in his eye no less pronounced than that of the sun-kissed water as it tumbled over the boulders nearby.

'I wonder why. Surely they didn't think you'd lie about a thing like that.'

'I never lie. I may not tell the truth all the time, but I never lie,' Guy said, suddenly serious.

'No, it was a joke. I didn't mean . . . you know I didn't.'

'I'm sorry. Throwback. Something that happened a long time ago.'

She didn't ask and he didn't tell her.

'Are you ready? Let's pack these things away and move on,' he said, and soon they managed to shake off the awkward moment in the pleasure of their surroundings. After about half an hour Guy stopped and pointed.

'There's a rather nice area over there.

I saw it the other day but I didn't go over; I wasn't wearing the right shoes. Today, however . . . You game?'

'Only if you stay with both feet on the bank until I get to the other side.'

'I'm saddened you don't trust me,' Guy said, trying to look hurt and failing miserably.

'Of course I trust you. I'm just hedging my bets.'

'Okay, then. You first.'

Honey managed the boulders with no trouble, though she did have a little wobble in the middle.

'Your turn.'

'On my way.'

Only it didn't quite work out like that. For some reason — Guy blamed it on the backpack — he lost his balance and ended up in the water. In itself this wasn't much of a disaster, aside from the ignominy of falling in. However, in trying to save himself he got his foot caught underneath a rock and twisted his ankle.

'Ow! That really hurts.'

At first Honey thought he was joking in an attempt to draw her back into the river, but then she realised when she saw the colour drain from his face that he was in real pain. 'Hang on, Guy. Don't try to move. I'll come and give you a hand.'

Honey tried very hard to maintain her own balance but in the end they both got very wet indeed. She managed to dislodge his trapped foot and they stumbled to the bank.

'Can I take off your shoe and have a look?' she asked.

'It's probably better to leave it alone. I don't think it's too bad, really; it's just that the shock caught me out for a minute. If we remove the shoe the likelihood is it will swell up, and it's a long way back to the car. Do you drive? I'm not sure I'll be able to.'

In all her life Honey had never driven anything as grand as Guy's car. However she did hold a licence, and it seemed there would be no alternative. She didn't know whether to be excited or terrified, but there was no point in telling him about her misgivings. He had enough to worry about. She wasn't going to scratch the car anyway, was she?

'Of course I can drive. However, we're not out of the woods yet — literally. Is it very tender?'

'Not so tender that I'm willing to forego that picnic. Here, let's get this off me,' he said as he struggled to get the pack off his back.

Guy's colour had returned and it was obvious the injury, painful though it might be, wasn't very serious. Lunch was consumed with eagerness by both. There's nothing like a walk to work up an appetite. Honey had even thoughtfully brought a piece of chocolate fudge cake for Guy, which made him laugh, but it didn't stop him refusing to share it with her.

'Surely you brought some for yourself?'

'I didn't expect you to wolf down the whole lot.'

'Then you've forgotten how much I like chocolate fudge cake.'

'If I'd forgotten I wouldn't have brought it with me, would I?'

One up to Honey.

* * *

Somehow they made it back to the car without further mishap, although they did get their feet wet when they crossed the river again.

'Just as my socks had dried out as well.'

'You'd better put those other shoes on anyway if you're going to drive.'

She did and they drove home, Honey managing not to get a single scratch on the car and very much enjoying driving something with so much power.

'That was great fun,' she said as she pulled up outside the Grange. 'Thank you for a lovely day. I hope your ankle doesn't give you too much trouble.'

'You're welcome. It's much better since we've been in the car and I've kept my weight off it. Maybe we can do it again, when my ankle's better.'

'That would be lovely.'

'I'm sorry I can't walk you home.'

'That's okay. While I'm here I'll pop in and see my mother.'

'Okay, I'll go and see if I can rustle up a dry pair of socks.'

'That would be nice. I don't really want to squelch myself all the way home.'

★ ★ ★

Honey spent half an hour with Daisy in the day room, where most of the patients went when they weren't in their rooms. It was a nice room overlooking the garden, and because of the age of the house the doorways were wide enough to make for the easy wheelchair access some of the patients needed. Ramps had been put in to help.

'The sun's going down now, Mum, but it's been a beautiful day. Have you been looking out of the window?'

Daisy pointed. 'At the garden? Of course.'

There were tears in Honey's eyes as she got up to leave, tears of anger that Guy was being so high-handed in his treatment of the residents. Her mother was so content in these beautiful surroundings. As she walked into the reception area he came out of a side room proffering dry socks. He didn't get quite the reaction he'd been expecting.

'How can you, Guy? She's happy here. They're all happy here. How can you even think about taking that away from them?'

She stormed out, leaving him holding the socks. Guy turned away sadly, thinking, *Two steps forward three steps back.*

10

Suzie was both pleased and amazed at the response to her article. It seemed the whole of Rills Ford was against the proposed new care home, and her celebrity had risen to such a height that people were stopping to talk to her in the street.

'You did absolutely the right thing, young lady. Thinks he can come back here and do what he likes with never a by-your-leave,' said one.

'It's about time somebody took a stand against those who are born with a silver spoon in their mouth and act as if the whole world belonged to them,' said another.

There were a lot of 'just like his mother' — type remarks which Suzie knew wasn't true, but which she wasn't given the opportunity to refute because, once they got started, people did so like to offer their opinion. With a pang of guilt she thought she probably wouldn't have done so anyway. She wasn't keen to protect Guy, not because she didn't like him, but because she cared passionately about her environment and she truly believed what she was doing was for the best. Suzie was secretly amused by the attitude of some of her assenters and told Honey.

'All these accusations about wealth and everything coming easily; anyone would think people here were on the breadline instead of living in a pretty affluent area surrounded by upper-middle-class folk. Don't quote me on that.'

'I hate to say it, Suzie — and don't you quote me either — but most are small-town people with small-town minds.'

Suzie took out her reporter's pad and pencil and began to write. 'Would you mind saying that again? I'd like to get it just right.'

'Don't you dare,' Honey said, laughing. 'Seriously, Suzie, I'm more than grateful to you for what you've done, but I can't help feeling that some of the people in Rills Ford are making a scapegoat of Guy, rather than concentrating on the real issue of the care home.'

'You're right, of course, but anything that carries this campaign forward is good enough for me.'

Honey knew her friend well enough to know that Suzie's motives were honourable, but she couldn't help thinking it wasn't doing her career any harm either. If push came to shove, would Suzie's principles outweigh her craving for success? As far as Honey was concerned, the only pushing and shoving involved her mother, from one place to another. 'And I'm not having it, Suzie. Not if I can do anything to stop it.'

* * *

Honey thought Guy's mini-patisserie idea only proved what a thoughtful man he really was, which left her at even more of a loss to understand why he was being so high-handed about the Grange. *Okay, I know it's his home, but if he's managed without it for fourteen years, why the hell doesn't he build something for himself in the grounds instead?* She knew she was being unreasonable. Whatever she might think about her mother and the rest of them, it was his ancestral home. Alexandra had always given people to understand that the tenuous noble link came through her line, when in fact it was her husband's. While she didn't give a toss about anyone but herself — unless they were rich or famous or both — her son had inherited something of the responsibilities of noblesse oblige and Honey recognised this. Aside from the monstrosity she believed he was planning to build, she had no illusions that he was in it for the money. Guy would always try to do the right thing. She'd recognised it in the boy on several occasions when he'd got Basil out of a scrape, and she knew it in the man.

No matter what she thought about him, though, her mother had no one but Honey to look out for her. The conflict within her was pulling her in different directions, so on Monday evening she 'lost' herself in her baking, experimenting with sizes and shapes and fillings in an effort to make her pastries different from anything else that might be available. By the end of the week, after working all hours, she'd achieved something she was satisfied with.

On Sunday morning she baked a complete batch of assorted patisserie, decorating each little cake with a marzipan bee, and took them to the Grange to show Guy. She hadn't seen him all week. He hadn't been to the tearooms and she hadn't given herself an evening off to go to the Rose and Crown, the main centre of the town for socialising. She tried to persuade herself she hadn't missed him.

'Honey, these are truly magnificent.'

She smiled, tried to look demure, but failed and grinned at him. 'I am quite pleased with them myself. I did drawings of most of them first so that I could see what I was aiming for.'

'Maybe you're the one who should have been an architect.'

Oops. Wrong thing to say. Honey's smile fled. Guy was inwardly kicking himself, but he was honestly more impressed than he'd expected to be. Here was a real talent, and it gave him an idea, though he realised he'd have to tread carefully as he was obviously prone to putting his foot in it.

'Have you seen Daisy yet? It's nearly teatime. Maybe we could go and join the residents and see what they think, though it's a shame to ruin such artistry by eating them. Maybe I'll just . . . '

She slapped his hand away as he reached towards the tray, but the smile was back in place. 'Oh no you don't.

These aren't for you. No I haven't seen her yet, and yes it seems like a good time to try them out.'

'Here, let me carry them.'

'As if.'

'Don't be silly. I need both hands to hold the tray. They'll be safer if I take them.'

The looks of delight were everything Honey needed to reward her for the effort she'd made, because she was truly tired. She thought Daisy looked tired as well, and took Betty to one side to see if she'd noticed.

'Yes, she's been like this for the last couple of days. We're keeping an eye on her and we'll call the doctor in if we think there's an underlying cause.'

'I feel so guilty. I've been rushing back to work every evening and I didn't even notice.'

'Well if these are the results of your labours, I can see why you might have been preoccupied. You've put a lot of thought into the presentation and the one I tasted just melted in my mouth.'

Betty's practised eye looked keenly at Honey without her even realising, at the beginnings of little worry lines in the corners of her eyes.

'Look, try not to be anxious, which I realise is a silly thing to say because I know you can't help it. It may just be one of those things that fly around at this time of year. No one's come down with anything yet, but I always dread it. You can bet your bottom dollar if one gets it they all will.'

Honey knew there was little that escaped Betty and trusted her implicitly to care for her charges. She went to talk to Daisy again, but as her mother was hardly responsive she got up to leave when Guy said, 'I'd like to talk before you go, if you have time.'

'Yes, of course. Here?'

'In the study. This way.'

Honey followed him out into the large hallway with its magnificent divided staircase and shuddered at the thought of the modern monstrosity she believed Guy was planning to build close by. Here all was peaceful, the surroundings speaking of warmth and comfort, the occasional pieces of furniture and beautiful hangings in the gallery window giving hint to a more elegant age than the one in which they now lived. Guy's study was a fairly large room, big enough for a desk even though it was huge, and a couple of armed leather chairs as well as a sofa. The wood panelling completed the picture. This was a gentleman's room.

'Please sit down,' he said, gesturing to one of the chairs. 'I'm a bit apprehensive. I'm not quite sure how you're going to take this.'

Her curiosity aroused, Honey did as she was asked and sat with her hands folded demurely in her lap, and waited.

'They went down well, didn't they, the pastries?' Guy said, and she thought he was prevaricating until he went on without waiting for an answer. 'I can see there's a lot of work involved and therefore a lot of time. Have you ever thought of going into business?'

'I am in business.'

'Another business.'

'Come on, Guy, you can see it's all I can do keeping up with the commitments I have already.'

'I can, but I can also see the possibilities here.'

'Possibilities?'

'You told me you have help at the Honey Bun in the busy season. What if you had help all the time?'

'I can't afford it. Even now I'm doing my best to make ends meet.' She hated having to admit it but it was, after all, a fact.

'You'll agree there's nothing in Rills Ford that even approaches what you've brought here this afternoon.' It was a statement, not a question. He plunged on in. 'If we were to have dedicated premises, could you produce these in quantity? Enough for the tearooms here and to supply other markets?'

Honey heard everything Guy said, but there was one word she got particularly hung up on. 'We?'

'I'm willing to do the short-term part. Find a suitable place or build one if necessary.'

She thought this typically high-handed of him but refrained from saying so, eager to hear what was coming next.

'I'll fund it and you can tell me exactly what you need. Then — ' He paused and smiled. ' — I'll leave it to you to do the hard work.'

'I don't want to work for you, Guy.'

'Nobody's asking you to. This will be an equal partnership. What do you say, Honey? Are you ready for a new adventure?'

Honey's face was inscrutable, but beneath the surface her emotions were in turmoil. She'd carried the burden for so long it had never occurred to her there might be a way to lighten the load of responsibility at least, if not of work, and she'd never been frightened of hard work. There was far too much to consider for her to give an answer immediately, but Guy's eyebrow had arched when he'd asked the question and he was grinning now as he waited for her to take in what he'd said. She was about to hedge when the door burst open and Betty came rushing in.

'You'd better come quickly, Honey. It's Daisy.'

11

Honey was out of the study before Betty had time to finish the sentence. She rushed to her mother's room only to find it empty and Betty, much slower behind her, calling out that Daisy was still in the sitting room. Racing back again she found Daisy still in the same chair, but the change was considerable. One side of her face had dropped and her left arm was hanging uselessly. Her eyes were open but were not focussing, and she seemed to be completely unaware of her surroundings. Honey dropped to her knees and took the limp hand in her own, looking first into her mother's face and then at Betty with the question to which she already knew the answer.

'We've called for an ambulance. Ah, yes, I can hear it coming now.'

'A stroke?'

'I believe so, Honey.'

'Why didn't you call me straight away?' It sounded like an accusation but Betty knew it was fear.

'I did, as soon as I'd made the call. You'll go with her, in the ambulance?'

'Of course. Should I talk to her; try to make her understand?'

'Just hold her hand and speak gently. She may hear; she may take comfort, even if she doesn't show it.'

Honey looked up at Guy, standing a little distance away, wishing he could do something to help. He smiled in what he hoped was a reassuring way and helped Honey to her feet as the ambulance crew came in. He was still supporting her arm as they followed the wheelchair out to the waiting vehicle.

'Would you like me to come with you?'

'Yes, but I think it might be a bit crowded in there,' she said ruefully, pointing to where Daisy was being lifted gently into the ambulance. 'Can I call you later, when I know more?'

'Of course; any time, day or night. Honey . . . ' He paused before continuing. 'You're not alone.'

The tears came as she climbed up to sit beside her mother, to hold her hand, to utter words that she hoped would comfort. The doors closed and the paramedic handed her a tissue.

'It won't be long. We'll soon have her settled in hospital. It's important to catch these things as early as possible, but she'll be in the best place in the best hands.'

★　★　★

The next few days Honey moved as if in a dream. Working on automatic, she kept the shop open only at teatime. She was touched by the response of the community, who rallied round, many offering to bake for her, though in truth the only time she was able to relax was in the evenings after she came home from the hospital. Making cakes was such a part of her, she could do it almost with her eyes closed. Customers flooded in during the afternoon; some she was only used to seeing intermittently, while Mrs Worthington came every day as usual. All wanted to help in whatever way they could, and if that meant the intake of a few more calories so be it.

Honey spent her mornings and the early part of each evening sitting with her mother. There was little improvement but neither did she get any worse. Once Honey was convinced she could feel a slight pressure from the hand she was holding, that there was more understanding in her mother's eyes, but these were fleeting impressions and though she reported them to the nurse she began to doubt herself when it didn't happen again. Guy insisted on acting as her escort every time she went.

'I can't ask you to be my chauffeur every day twice a day.'

'I don't remember hearing you ask, and it's nice to feel useful. I'm in the habit of working and this indolence doesn't suit me at all.'

She accepted gratefully. In fact, things would have been considerably harder for her without his help. Four days after Daisy had the stroke, Basil arrived with his family. Guy took Honey to the airport to collect them. Even the worry about her mother couldn't take away her excitement at seeing her brother again, and meeting Lucy and Tom for the first time was like reacquainting herself with them. Thanks to Skype they were all familiar to each other, but nothing could have taken the place of the real live hugs they all exchanged. It was an airport scene that is played at any airport every day all over the world, the coming together of family and friends. Tom flung himself at Guy like he was an old friend, which of course he was.

'How is she, Hon? Has there been any change?' Basil asked his sister.

'Minimal, I think, but I'm hoping

now you're here it will make a difference.'

'Can we go straight to the hospital?'

'Probably not a good idea, Bas; not after the journey you've just had.'

By this time Guy had extricated himself and Honey fell to her knees to meet her nephew on his own level. 'I've been so looking forward to seeing you, Tom. My goodness, what a big boy you are.'

'I'm five! This is my mummy.'

'I've been looking forward to meeting you too, Lucy, just not under these circumstances.'

'And I've been planning next year's trip for so long, looking forward to the time Daisy and Basil could be together again for a while, when she could meet Tom, and now . . .'

'Now we'll get you home and give you a cup of tea and some time to catch up with yourself before we visit Mum.'

Guy, overhearing the comment, smiled and said: 'Honey's cure for everything, a cup of tea. It was the first thing she offered me when I arrived too.'

Having successfully relieved some of the tension, Guy mounted Tom on his shoulders while still managing to manoeuvre a laden trolley with one hand, and led the small group to the car. Basil, his wife on one side and his sister on the other, followed with a second trolley. The shared load eased the burden and, for the time being at least, their spirits were lifted.

★   ★   ★

'You haven't changed anything, Hon!'

She was pretty sure her big brother had tears in his eyes. Although he hadn't been away as long as Guy, it was four years since last he'd left Australia.

'We're creatures of habit here. I even had comments when I added the bee logo, though fortunately they were all complimentary. I'd probably have lost half my customers if I'd changed the décor. I can hear them now: 'What, the old place wasn't good enough for you?

We don't like change in Rills Ford, you know. I bet Daisy would have something to say.''

The mention of her mother in a joke that was meant to lighten things only caused the mood to change immediately; and tired though they were after the journey, Basil and his family insisted on going to see Daisy straight away.

'If we stay here we'll only fall asleep,' Lucy said to Honey while the men took the luggage upstairs. 'It'll help get us back into phase. Anyway, he wants to see for himself.'

'Yes, of course he does. Is that all right with you, Guy? Do you mind taking us again?' Honey asked him as they came back into the tearooms.

'No problem.'

★ ★ ★

Lucy and Honey hung back from the bed as father and son approached, but it wasn't Basil who provoked a reaction in Daisy, it was Tom. The boy was the image of his dad, and whether she was for the moment living in the past or just that his excitement got through to her they couldn't tell.

'Hello, Gran. It's me. I've come in a plane to see you, all the way from 'stralia.'

The lifeless hand that Basil had taken in his own twitched; something of a spark appeared in Daisy's eyes as she turned her head to look at the child. There was no wondering for Honey this time if it was wishful thinking. The reaction was small but significant and it didn't need Basil to say 'She tried to squeeze my fingers, I'm sure of it' for them all to know that something had changed.

Guy rushed out to get the nurse, who smiled when she saw Tom sitting on the bed, his hand gripped in Daisy's good one.

'Ow, Gran, that hurts.'

Lucy moved forward and praised the small boy.

'It's because she's so pleased to meet you at last, Tom. Aren't you glad now we didn't have to wait until you were six like we thought?'

'I'm delighted to see you all here, and even more delighted at the effect you're having on my patient, but I think maybe another five minutes or so and then leave her to rest. It's been a big day for her.'

Basil had been shocked at the sight of his mother looking so pale against the sheets. If it hadn't been for her reaction and the reassurance of Honey and the nurse, he'd have been in despair. As it was, he began to hope there might be some improvement. The last time he'd been in England Daisy wasn't coping as well as could be expected with her widowhood and she hadn't yet moved to The Grange. Tom was just a baby at the time, and he and Lucy didn't want to put him or themselves through the ordeal of such a long journey, so Basil had made the trip to see his mother alone. The change in her since then had frightened him; she seemed somehow shrunken. Guy, who knew how hard his friend was struggling, tried to break his mood.

'It's going to be a bit cramped with all of you at the Honey Bunny, Bas. How do you feel about letting Tom stay with me at the Grange while you're here?'

Basil allowed himself to be distracted and Tom was thrilled with the idea. Guy was an old friend and had been a source of treats back home. It was decided, though, that for the first night he would stay with his parents in case there was any problem with his body clock adjusting. In any case the boy suddenly wilted and his father carried him up to bed.

'He didn't even wake when I undressed him. I don't think I'll be far behind him either.'

12

There's something about living in a small community. There can be lots of back-biting and attitude. Small factions can war with each other; reputations can be made or lost because of malicious gossip. When one of their number was in trouble, though, the whole lot of them — well most, anyway — pulled together, beginning in this case with another article written by Suzie in the *Rills Ford Post*.

Another Old Rills Fordian Returns to the Fold

Not long ago I used these pages to draw your attention to a planning proposal by renowned architect, Guy Ffoulkes. Whether or not you are one of those who agree, your response was overwhelming. This time I would like to invoke your help for something that requires much more than signing a piece of paper. One of our own is in trouble. Daisy Bunting recently suffered a stroke and is at present in hospital. There can be few of us who haven't in the past been the recipient of her comfort and advice which often came in words as well as in cake. Her son Basil has rushed with his family from Australia to be by her side. Little Tom Bunting, I am told, sparked a reaction in Daisy and we can all only hope that with time her condition will improve. Time is the important word here. The Buntings are spending as much of it as they can at Daisy's bedside but Honey, her daughter, has a business to run and, as we all know businesses don't run themselves, many small ones are at risk. While I know several of you have already rallied round, I am using these pages to ask for a greater involvement so the family can be together at this difficult time.

There is no way Honey will relinquish the baking, which she does in the evening, to anyone else, but I know she would appreciate having her days free to be at the hospital. Having her children around her could be a major factor in Daisy's progress. I ask you therefore to join a rota to man the Honey Bun Tearooms during opening hours. For those of you unable to work, perhaps your contribution could be to increase your visits to this important establishment in our community. Come on, we all like to indulge in a pastry or two occasionally. If you are able to help, please phone or email me and I will take on the responsibility of organising a timetable. If we are not for each other then who are we for? On Honey's behalf, because I know she would

*not ask for herself, please contact
me and prove why it is I am so
proud to be a part of this
community.*

Suzie was astonished when on
showing the copy to Jack, and completely out of character, he picked her
up and twirled her around. Embar-
rassed by this show of sentiment and
what he considered to be his own
unprofessional attitude, he jumped
away as the colour rose through his
neck into his face and ears. Suzie
thought it delightful but made a
pretence of straightening her clothing
while he regained his composure.

'I'm sorry, Suzie. I got a bit carried
away. It's just that it's wonderful to
think the *Post* can be instrumental in
helping our own.'

'Erm, I take it that means it's okay to
run the piece?' she asked him, the
reason she'd shown it to him in the first
place.

'Not only that, but . . . well, the

paper takes its name from this town. It is our raison d'être, so don't just run it, Suzie. We'll give it the front page. Show them that at the *Rills Ford Post* we care about our neighbours.'

Suzie went back to her own office walking on air. She could still feel the strength of Jack's arms where he'd held her. What she wasn't aware of was that he was suddenly seeing her in a completely different light. She would have been more than happy had she known.

★ ★ ★

'How long will you be able to stay, Bas?'

'I've taken two weeks' leave with the option to extend to three. It doesn't look like Mum's going to get better that quickly, does it? If at all.'

'I'm not so sure. Don't be too quick to judge. The difference already is amazing. Okay, I'm convinced sometimes she thinks Tom is you, but that's understandable given the circumstances.'

'Circumstances?'

'Before this happened she was already struggling with trying to mend broken bones. I worried occasionally when I saw her shoulders drop, when it seemed it was all a bit much for her. Nevertheless she seemed perfectly happy most of the time. Before she had this stroke I used to get really upset. Now I just wish she was like that again.'

Basil looked at his sister, realising for the first time what a burden she'd been carrying alone.

'It's all fallen on your shoulders, hasn't it? I didn't realise. When you're that far away you don't think. I'm so sorry, Honey. I wish I could have done more to help.'

'Well you're helping now; at least, Tom is. She seems so pleased to see him, I don't think it matters if any of the rest of us are there or not.'

'And there is some improvement,

isn't there, even in the few days we've been here.'

'No doubt about it.'

'Look, if I have to take extra time then that's what I'll do.'

'Let's take it a day at a time, Bas. Your job's on the line as well. You have a family to support. You can't stay away forever.'

Basil accepted the logic of what Honey was saying, but it didn't stop him feeling riddled with guilt.

* * *

There weren't many people who had the power to intimidate Guy, but his heart fell to his boots when he saw several suitcases standing in the hall of the Grange when he went home one day, leaving Daisy's family with her at the hospital. He'd promised to go back for them later. There was no doubting who the luggage belonged to, both from its design and quantity. Summoning up his courage, Guy went in search of Alexandra.

'Hello, Mother. This is a surprise. What are you doing here?'

'I've come home, darling.'

Guy winced at the 'darling' and the candy-sweet way the word was uttered. 'It isn't your home. It's mine. You live in France.'

'Not anymore. Your father has taken up with some floozy. Oh, Guy, I can't believe it. He was so horrible to me; not like him at all. He usually agrees with *everything* I say.'

Only for a peaceful life, Guy thought, but this wasn't the time to say so.

'He told me he wanted me to leave. That he'd had enough of being a satellite and now he wants to be his own star. That he'll make me a generous allowance but our marriage is over.'

At this point Alexandra dissolved into tears — not the false ones Guy had been so used to seeing when she dabbed at her eyes with a tissue while being careful not to disturb her beautifully applied make-up. This was real, and descended into sobs so heavy he could almost feel the pain in his own chest.

'If that's the case, why didn't you just take an apartment of your own in France?'

Alexandra looked shocked that he could even suggest such a thing. 'But everybody knows. I wouldn't have been able to hold my head up. No, coming home was my only option.'

'As I've already pointed out, Mother, this isn't your home and it isn't an option,' Guy said, but he could feel the ground slipping under his feet. He could hardly turf her out into the street. 'Have you thought about taking a room at the Rose and Crown? Since you left it's been converted into a high class gastro-pub. The rooms have all had a make-over, each en suite and beauti-fully done. Luxury in every detail, and I know it's well thought of. The chef is superb. I know; I've eaten there a couple of times already since I came back.' He wasn't hopeful but it was worth a try.

'I couldn't possibly. They hate me there. Anyway, why can't I stay here?'

'There aren't any spare rooms, Mother. The Grange is a residential care home and every room is occupied.'

He saw her cringe, and knew it was the idea of the old house being used for such circumstances. She was perfectly capable of being a snob about its heritage even if it wasn't her heritage.

'Yes, I know. I've already seen Betty Grant. She's got a bit above her station if you ask me. A housekeeper.'

'She isn't a housekeeper anymore. She's the manager, and nothing happens here without her knowledge or approval.'

Guy was backed into a corner. Much as he'd liked to have done, he couldn't put his mother in a hotel. Ultimately he knew he'd have to help her find a new home. He just hoped it wouldn't be in Rills Ford. In the meantime, the way he saw it he only had one choice. It worried him, though, and he'd have to talk to Betty about it. He was sure he could rely on her common sense to recognise the situation for what it was, but all the same there was bound to be trouble ahead.

'Okay, Mother, until you decide what to do you can have my room. It has to be short-term though. In the meantime, *I'll* move to the Rose and Crown.'

'Oh thank you, darling, thank you. I knew I could rely on you.'

Guy left Alexandra in the study where they'd been talking, picked up her luggage and took it to his room. After that he went in search of Betty to break the bad news. All things considered she took it fairly well, but she too was a force to be reckoned with and no longer in a position where she had to be deferential to her former employer. There was one thing Guy hadn't thought of, though, until Betty asked: 'What are you going to do about Tom?'

13

Suzie's call for help produced results in much the same ratio as had her petition, though this time the focus was on the pros rather than the cons. There were the few who asked, 'What have they ever done for me?' But mostly the Buntings were held in affection by their neighbours. Aside from that, the very real risk of one of their businesses going under was something they would do what they could to avoid. Although they lived to some extent in a fairly closed community, they were not entirely unaware of and certainly not immune to larger events happening outside their immediate sphere.

'It's bad enough having that great big supermarket next to the industrial estate just outside of town,' Mrs Worthington was heard to remark.

Always practical, Mary Simpson was

known to have replied that the hated supermarket was keeping several of the local inhabitants employed. Nor was the population averse to using its facilities when it suited them. Rills Ford fell somewhere between being a large town and a small town; small enough to have that quintessential feeling that made visitors know they had escaped to the country, and large enough to have a high street that supported a variety of shops that catered not just for its residents but was interesting enough to draw people, many of whom returned if not every year then certainly on a regular basis. The warm-coloured stone and the period architecture which featured in many a tourist guide was one of the reasons there had been so much dissention about Guy's plans for the Grange. Built in material garnered from the local quarry, it was a local attraction and folk didn't want to see it changed. Had they taken the trouble to visit the planning office themselves, they might have been reassured, but instead they had jumped to conclusions.

★ ★ ★

Honey, independent and self-sufficient Honey, shed a quiet tear in the privacy of her bedroom. Why would anyone want to leave this place where neighbours were friends and acquaintances became like neighbours? Suzie had taken action quickly, and it was in no small part thanks to her that Honey wasn't on the verge of collapse. Thanks to her and thanks to Guy. Honey had to acknowledge that without him she'd have been at her wits' end. Even supporting Basil's spirits and taking the weight off his parents by engaging with Tom were sufficient in themselves to make a huge difference.

She'd been dismayed when she'd learned of Alexandra's return. She'd feared her as a child and was in awe of her as an adult. Nothing her common

145

sense told her changed that. When Guy told her he'd moved out of the Grange, her first reaction was antipathy towards his mother, her second what to do with Tom. Guy had been quite right when he'd said it would be crowded at home, and though she'd never admit it, she was finding it difficult to cope with Lucy and Basil sharing her bathroom and other facilities.

'Tom can come with me. There's plenty of room.'

'I can just imagine Bas, or Lucy for that matter, allowing their son to live over a pub.'

'It's a hotel, Honey. Families stay there all the time.'

Whether it was charm on Guy's part or desperation on that of Tom's parents, it was decided the boy should stay with his godfather.

The hospital didn't allow visiting before lunch so, with more help than she could possibly have wished for, Honey took to baking in the mornings, thus leaving her evenings free for the first time in her adult working life.

'Tom and I would be delighted if you would join us for dinner this evening, Honey.'

'You and Tom?'

'It was his idea.'

'He's obviously fed up with you already and needs a bit of light relief.'

'And you wouldn't want to let him down, would you?'

'Of course not. What about Lucy and Bas?'

'That's not very polite. I invite you for a meal and immediately you want other people to join us. I'm sending them in a taxi to the Grapes. I thought it might be nice if they had some time on their own.'

'That's so nice of you, Guy. What a lovely thought.'

'Not at all. I want you to myself for a change.'

Is he flirting with me?

'And Tom of course,' she countered.

'Naturally and Tom of course.

'Then I'd love to. Thank you.'

★ ★ ★

Guy dropped all the Buntings off at the hospital and went back to the Grange to pick up a few things that he'd forgotten to take with him to the Rose and Crown. He'd liked to have been able to avoid his mother, but as she had little to do with her time she was on the lookout for him.

'Darling,' she greeted him, putting Guy immediately on the alert. 'Darling, I was wondering if you'd like to take me out for a drive this afternoon. We could find one of those nice quaint places for tea in the country; have a little chat. After all, we haven't seen much of each other lately, have we?'

'I'm sorry, Mother, I can't. I have to pay a visit to the Planning Department to clear up one or two small points.'

'Couldn't you do that another time? It would be nice for us to spend some time together. In any case I'm so bored.'

The truth at last.

'I'm sorry, no. If you're bored, why don't you go into the lounge and talk to some of the residents? It's always nice for them to see a new face, much as they enjoy the familiar ones.'

Alexandra looked shocked; almost as if he'd said something rude. 'Those people,' she said with emphasis. 'What on earth would I have to say to them?' she asked, putting the stress on the last word.

Probably nothing good, Guy thought, but it wouldn't have been politic to say so. He tried side-tracking. 'Have you had any ideas about where you'd like to go from here?'

She patted the sofa next to her in a manner meant to be inviting. Guy realised he'd have to give her some time but sat opposite her, terrified she might pat his knee or something equally revolting.

'I know you're planning on giving this place a makeover and I understand it will take some time to build a new place for those people.' *I wonder if she knows how condescending she sounds.* 'But when it's done, well, you'll have the whole place to yourself again. I could move in here with you.'

'No!'

It probably sounded a bit harsher than he'd meant it to, but in any case he knew he needed to be firm. He couldn't afford to give her the tiniest fraction of an inch.

'Why not?' The sharpness was back in her voice. It was certainly preferential to the wheedling.

'Because I'm far too old to live with my mother, for one thing.'

'It's my home.'

'No it isn't, and you were very ready to take my money and run when I bought it from Dad.' She took a deep breath and was about to speak again, but Guy stood up and raised his hand. 'There is no point in you trying to pursue this, Mother. The answer will always be no and you'll only distress yourself if you persist. If you'll excuse me, I have to go out now.'

He let out a deep breath as he entered the hall, stopping only to apologise to Betty on his way to pack his stuff. 'If it's too much for you, Betty, tell me. I'll get rid of her somehow.'

'Don't you worry, Guy. I can deal with the likes of your mother now she doesn't have my livelihood hanging over my head. If you want some advice, though, come and see me when you have a few minutes. I've one or two suggestions.'

Clutching at the proffered straw, Guy said, 'Yes, I'll do that. Thank you.'

* * *

It didn't take Guy long to put his few remaining things into a bag and drop them back at the hotel. The bulk of his belongings were in storage, waiting for the time he could settle down properly, and now he had an added reason to hope that would happen as quickly as possible. It was obvious to him that Honey only regarded him as a friend (men are so blind) and he was sure if he was to have any chance with her at all he would have to move very slowly. Guy was as apprehensive as anyone on their first date but was looking forward to spending the evening, a proper evening, having dinner with Honey. Tom, he was sure, would be an asset rather than an encumbrance. In any case, he was inordinately fond of the boy and beginning to wish he had children of his own. He had all the innocence and refreshing honesty of a five-year-old, so it was a pleasure to be with him.

Once Guy had started making a name for himself, people had fawned on him and he'd mistakenly thought their adulation was friendship. As a child who had so long been deprived of affection, he didn't recognise that the sycophancy was much the same as fans would give a film star. By the time he'd learned that it was not who he was but what he was that was attracting people to him, he'd become disillusioned and more introverted than ever — not that an observer would have known. His social skills were honed and his company sought. Any gathering of which he was a part was guaranteed to have some modicum of success.

To him, though, it was all hollow and was eventually the cause of him heading back to Rills Ford. He may not have had a happy childhood there but his home, the place itself, was a stronghold in his mind and he resolved to turn it into his own personal fortress — after he'd built a new facility for its residents. The arrival of his mother was an added complication and he knew that trouble lay ahead, but he was strong enough now to deal with it. Doing so kindly could prove to be difficult. Though he didn't hold her in affection, he was not an unkind man.

He scratched his head and went off to collect the Buntings from the hospital. 'How is she today? Any change?' he asked Lucy while Bas and Honey were saying their goodbyes.

'She squeezed my hand really really

hard today,' said Tom, who had heard the question. He had been persuaded that it was a sign of his grandmother's attachment to him and as such was proud of himself. 'Mummy says I'm helping more than anyone.'

'And I'm sure Mummy is right, but if you don't stop tugging on my sweater it isn't a squeeze of the hand you'll be getting from me. Come on, now. If you want to stay up for dinner we need to get you bathed and into some clean clothes. You do have clean clothes?'

Tom giggled. 'Of course I do.'

14

Guy dropped the three older Buntings at the teashop and took Tom back to the hotel for the promised bath. Meanwhile Honey spent much more time than usual preparing herself for . . . what? Was it a date? It could hardly be called that, not with her nephew being there as well. Mascara wand in hand, she paused in its application to realise that she couldn't actually remember the last time she'd been on a date. *For heaven's sake, you're nearly thirty years old. Stop acting like a teenager.* Oddly enough, though, she felt like a teenager; and there was a little place somewhere in the middle of her stomach that reminded her of that wonderful weaving and swooping starlings do before settling down to roost.

Guy was also taking extra care over his appearance and was sufficiently honest to know he was out to impress if he could. He hadn't told Honey the complete truth when he'd said the idea of dinner for three had been Tom's. It was something he'd planted subtly in the boy's mind and he felt almost guilty when Tom said, 'You didn't think of asking Auntie Honey for dinner. It was me.' But he gave him credit and praised him.

Tom was very excited — overly in fact — and Guy was a little bit doubtful now about his idea to keep him up so late. But he needn't have worried. Tom adopted the attitude of a fifty- rather than a five-year-old, studying the choices on the menu (after Guy helped him read them), discussing the merits of this one, the demerits of that. In the end he chose a pasta dish, and neither Honey nor Guy was optimistic about him maintaining the cleanliness of his clothes. But they'd underestimated their charge, and both were hugely entertained by his contributions to the conversation. Until, that was, the moment when a neighbour leaned over from an adjacent table and said to Tom, 'What a good little boy you are,' before turning to Honey and Guy. 'Are you two getting in some practice then, looking after children?'

Honey was overcome with embarrassment as Tom looked first at one and then the other.

'Are you having a baby?'

'No, of course not, Tom. We're not even married.' Realising that the hole was getting deeper, she began to flounder, but her rescue came from an unexpected quarter.

'My mummy's having a baby.'

There was a stunned silence from both Honey and Guy before she said: 'That's wonderful. I didn't know.'

'Oh, I forgot; I wasn't supposed to say.'

Guy, who had been uncharacteristically quiet for a few moments, reassured him immediately. 'Don't worry. Your secret is safe with us.'

Honey jumped up to give her nephew

a hug, and that was how she and not he ended up with pasta all over her clothes.

* * *

Lucy and Basil were having a wonderful time at the Grapes. It wasn't often they had a chance to be alone for what seemed to them both to be a romantic dinner for two. After they'd ordered their meal Basil held his wife's hands across the table.

'You look beautiful, Luce. Pregnancy suits you. I remember with Tom, you were glowing then just as you are now.'

She didn't argue with him; why would she? She just smiled back serenely and returned the pressure on her hands.

'I was a bit worried; you know, bringing you all this way.'

'I know you were, but you see I'm fine. I wish Daisy was in better health, but it's been lovely meeting Honey and seeing Guy again. He haunted the house so much when he was in Oz that I didn't realise how much he'd become a part of our lives until he'd gone. I missed him.'

'He's been a part of my life for as long as I can remember. I used to think he was looking after me. Well, he was looking after me, but I didn't know then that I was doing the same for him. You wouldn't believe how cold his mother was.'

'Oh yes I would. You've told me enough times and he's hinted as much to me himself. Poor little boy.'

For a moment she looked troubled and he knew she was thinking of Tom and their loving home and feeling sad for the boy Guy used to be.

'You'll probably have the doubtful pleasure of meeting Alexandra soon now she's come back to Rills Ford.'

'I can't wait,' she said, the irony plain to hear.

The waitress came and lit the candle on their table and Lucy watched her progress as she did the same around the restaurant. One table had a single specimen rose on it.

'Isn't that Suzie, Honey's friend? Looks like a cosy little tête-à-tête over there.'

Basil looked over his shoulder and waved.

'Yes and she's with Jack Jennings, her boss. Not that it looks like a work dinner, and certainly not with that rose.'

Suzie waved back but she was by no means pleased to have been seen on this, her first date with Jack, the one she'd been anticipating for what seemed like years. *Actually it is years*, she thought. Somehow, after all this time, Jack had suddenly seen Suzie not as an employee but as an attractive young woman whom he felt he'd rather like to get to know better — away from the office.

* * *

Back at the Rose and Crown, Tom had suddenly become very quiet and a little bit pale.

'Time for bed, young man. Come on, I'll carry you up on my shoulders.' Guy didn't think Tom would submit lightly to being carried up in his arms, so this was the best alternative he could think of. 'Will you wait here, Honey? We can have coffee if you wouldn't mind ordering it. I shouldn't be long.'

She looked around her, thinking how nice it was to have a proper evening out. She couldn't even remember the last time. Since her father had died and her mother had become more dependent on her, albeit somewhat grudgingly, there really hadn't been much opportunity. Suddenly she felt — not resentful, that was far too strong a word — regretful; that was it. Time had gone by without her even noticing, and she'd missed a lot.

Guy was back before she had time to start feeling sorry for herself and they spent the rest of the evening talking small talk before Honey said, 'It's okay. I'll walk home. It's only across the road.'

'I don't feel too comfortable with

that, but I must admit I'd feel less comfortable leaving the building when Tom's supposed to be in my charge.'

'It's nice you take your responsibilities so seriously,' Honey said, smiling because she meant it.

'I'd hate the little chap to wake up and call and for me not to be there. There's a gadget in reception that will signal if he wakes up, and I'd sooner be here in case that happens.'

They stood up, neither sure what to do next. They could hardly shake hands, and anything else was shaky ground for both, though neither knew it about the other.

'I've had a wonderful evening, Guy. Thank you.'

She leaned up, kissed his cheek, turned and left before he could see the colour flare up in hers.

* * *

The next morning Guy took a sleepy Tom with him to the Grange, where he had some paperwork to do before collecting the family after lunch to take them to see Daisy. It had already become a routine, and one he enjoyed, since it made him feel useful. Tom was doing a great job of entertaining the residents, quite happy to talk to them and not the least put out if they didn't respond, so Guy decided to leave him there as daily visits to the hospital were tedious for a child of his age.

Lucy, still in a rosy glow from her romantic evening the night before, was quite pleased to have a little break from her bouncy boy. Daisy, who was making steady progress, seemed to be looking around for him but settled immediately without any obvious untoward cffcct. Such was Daisy's improvement that the hospital had said she might be able to return home soon. They were unable to make any promises but the prognosis was good.

'It's possible she'll be better off in her own environment,' the doctor said, and

Honey couldn't help looking across at Guy. This raised her earlier concerns all over again about the upheaval for the residents of the Grange. Guy met her gaze steadily and she looked away — at her mother's face, at the doctor, anywhere but at him.

'We'll give her another couple of days here before we make any decision. This is just to prepare you.'

'For the worst, Doctor?' Basil asked.

'By no means, Mr Bunting. Just for the change in the situation.'

★   ★   ★

'Why don't you all come back to the Grange for a while? The tearooms are covered and it will give you a break. I know you'll start working if you go back now, Honey, and we have a wonderful choice of cakes made by a local talent. I think you'll enjoy them.'

Honey wasn't immune to this sort of flattery, and it would be more comfortable for all of them. Lucy and Basil naturally wanted to see Tom, so they all piled into the car and headed back.

★ ★ ★

'Betty, I wonder if you'd mind rustling up some tea and cakes for this hungry horde. Is Tom still in the residents' lounge?'

'Holding forth the last I saw of him.'

Guy went off in search of his godson while the others went into the study, a room large enough to serve as a personal sitting room. He appeared in the doorway a couple of minutes later with a big grin on his face.

'The little sod's done a runner. He's probably in the garden bending Henry's ear. I'll be back soon, once I've put him over my knees and given him a good spanking.'

He wasn't back quite as soon as they thought he'd be, and when he did return his face was the colour of paste. 'He's gone! Tom's gone! I can't find him anywhere.'

15

'You've checked the bedroom?' Basil said, jumping up.

'The whole place except the residents' rooms, and I guess he could be talking to one of them. It's a big house so it's best if we search systematically. We'll divide it up between us and meet back here in ten minutes. If we haven't found him by then . . . ' Guy paused, not wanting to but having to say, ' . . . I'll phone the police.'

It was fortunate his large frame was barring the doorway, or they'd all have shot out willy-nilly. He stopped them, organising them into in pairs. That way, as soon as they found Tom, one of the two could find and reassure the others while his or her partner looked after the boy in case he'd hurt himself or got lost and needed comforting. Guy had brought Betty and Henry, the gardener, back with him after his first failed mission. The Grange had three floors and they took one each, Honey and Henry, Lucy and Betty, Guy and Basil; that way at least one partner was familiar with the house. Guy had already calculated that it would be best for Lucy to be with the manager; she had a natural reassurance about her (that she wasn't feeling at the time) which would help control the dread that had fast risen up in Tom's mother's throat. He also wanted to be in a position to stop Basil rushing this way and that as panic took hold of him. The rest of the staff would be left to care for the residents.

Only Honey had a moment of hope as she heard a voice coming from one of the rooms. *He must be in here talking to Bertha*, she thought, entering the room next to her mother's vacant one. Hope was crushed when she found Bertha in quiet conversation with no one but herself. The group reassembled, only a couple of minutes later than planned.

'He can't have gone far. Henry here said he was talking to him in the garden barely an hour ago. I'd better make that call. There's a photo of Tom on my desk. The police will probably want that.'

Lucy and Basil looked bleak.

'Did anyone check the lift?' Betty asked, and when there was a negative response she rushed off to make sure he wasn't stuck in there. She added upon her return, 'I'll check the cleaning cupboard as well, and the store cupboards.'

'I'll have a look in the greenhouses and the potting shed,' said Henry, and he left the room at a run.

By the time they came back the police had arrived and were anxious to ask them some questions, as they'd been the last to see Tom apart from the residents, most of whom would have difficulty in giving any information even if they had it. Honey looked out of the window at the fading light. She took Guy to one side while Lucy and Basil were trying to help the police.

'It'll be dark soon. What if he's outside? He's only five; he'll be terrified.'

'We'll have to hope he thinks it's all a big adventure. Chin up, Honey, we'll find him,' Guy said with a confidence he didn't feel.

'The cellar! Did anyone check the cellar?' Betty called out. No one had, but again they drew a blank. There was an air of desperation in the room, by no means alleviated when the sergeant asked if Tom had ever run away before.

'What can we do, Officer? We can't just sit here and wait.'

'I'm afraid there's not much else you can do, other than search the grounds again if you're sure he's not in the house. Meanwhile we'll start making enquiries further afield.' The sergeant coughed before asking the next question. 'Would he have gone with someone? Erm, even a stranger?'

'As soon as anyone spoke to him they were his friend. Yes, yes, he would. Oh my God, you think he's been abducted?'

'We have to consider it as a possibility. I won't insult you by saying try not to worry, but there are set procedures in cases like this and we'll do everything we can to find him.'

*   *   *

None of them knew what to do with themselves. Inaction was the greatest torture.

'Why don't you and Basil go back home? Tom may have headed for the tearooms. It's a straight walk from here. He could be sitting on the doorstep waiting for you.'

They jumped at the suggestion and were out of the door almost before Honey had finished speaking. Guy looked at her. 'Do you think he might have done that?'

'I don't know, but at least it's given

them something to do. I wish I could think of something myself.'

'How long is it since you last saw him, Henry?'

Henry was feeling guilt-ridden. He'd been the last to talk to Tom and felt now that he should have made sure the boy had returned to the house. It wasn't true of course. The natural assumption was that he would have done so, but Guy knew how Henry was suffering and in his case it was multiplied several times over. Tom had been in his charge; his responsibility. If anyone was to blame it was him.

'No more'n two hours. He said his tummy was rumbling and he was off for his tea. I didn't know; I thought . . . '

'No one is criticising you, Henry. We'd have all thought the same. If anyone is at fault it's me. I shouldn't have left him unsupervised. It wasn't anybody else's responsibility to watch over him. You all had your own jobs to do here. Why don't you go home now? Your shift is finished and there's nothing more you can do here.'

'If it's all the same to you, sir, I think I'll take a wander up the lane, just in case. The lad might have gone for a walk and twisted his ankle or something.'

Guy smiled his gratitude, which made the old retainer feel much better. 'Have you got your mobile with you? You'll give us a call obviously, if you find him,' Guy added as Henry nodded his assent. He turned to Betty. 'You've got more than enough to do here, Betty. They'll all soon be screaming for their supper. I'm taking Honey in the car. If Henry's walking up the lane, we'll start a bit further along in case he's gone that way and gone beyond. Okay, Honey?' he said, turning to ask her, but she was already on her way out of the door.

* * *

Honey was feeling a cold chill that had nothing to do with the weather. She couldn't even begin to imagine what her brother and sister-in-law were going through. They'd sent a message to say they were back at the teashop and had drawn a blank but would be staying put just in case that was where Tom was heading. When he wasn't on the doorstep Basil had rushed across to the pub to see if he'd gone back there. Though no one had seen him, he even went as far as to look up in the room just in case Tom had crept in and was fast asleep while panic was going on all around. He wasn't, and Lucy could tell by his drooping shoulders long before he was near enough to tell her.

'He's five, Guy! Where could he have gone? Do you really think somebody could have taken him?' This was her worst dread, but she had to be reassured by Guy's answer.

'He was at the Grange. There wasn't anybody there who *could* have taken him. No, I'm convinced he's done what any five-year-old would have done. He knows he's all right, so it wouldn't occur to him that anyone else could think otherwise.'

'But where could he be?' Honey said, her fear evident in the raised level of her voice.

'That's what I'd like to know.'

'You see those interviews with the police on the television, where the family are there pleading for whoever has taken their child to return him. Is that what they'll be doing? Guy, I can't bear it.'

'I imagine it's normal procedure but you must remember, Honey, it was minutes rather than hours when we realised Tom was missing. We should be ahead of the game.'

'Ahead of the game! Game! This is my nephew we're talking about and it most certainly isn't a game.'

Guy chose to ignore this last remark and the note of hysteria he could hear in Honey's voice, and continued to drive very slowly up the lane with his headlights on full beam. There were times when he'd had to dip them. It wasn't a busy road but he managed to incur the anger of quite a few drivers as they waited impatiently for passing places. He could feel rather than see the glare as they overtook him. He didn't give a toss. Tom was the only thing that was important now. Every few yards they would stop and jump out, calling his name in case he'd fallen into a ditch or had encountered some other hazard. Progress was slow and fear forced a wedge between them rather than binding them together. Eventually Guy stopped the car and turned to look at Honey.

'He can't have got any further than this, not on his own two feet.'

'You're giving up?' she asked, incredulity in her voice and face.

'No, of course not. Just wondering what else we can try. Be realistic, Honey. He could never have walked this far on his own, not even in two hours.'

'We'd better go back then; see if anyone else has any news.' But they knew they wouldn't have. Everyone had a mobile phone. Nobody was going to wait to spread good news if it had come.

Honey's phone rang as they walked back into the Grange. It was Basil.

'They've found him! He's at the hospital.'

'Oh my God! Is he hurt? Has he had an accident? Is he all right, Basil? Is he going to be okay?'

She could hear her brother laughing. Presumably not hurt then.

'He went to see Mum. Can you believe it? He thought we might still be there so he went to meet us as he hadn't seen her today.'

'The hospital! But how did he get there? It's miles.'

'Can you come and get us? I'll tell you on the way. Meantime I'd better phone the police and tell them we've found him.'

Basil passed the good news around, not just to the police but to everyone else who'd been involved, and in no time they were bowling along the lane

Guy and Honey had crawled along a short time before.

'Apparently he got the bus.'

'He what?'

'That's what he told them at the hospital. He waited at the bus stop. Children travel free so presumably that's why the driver didn't query it when he got on. Just thought he must be a bit small for his age to be travelling on his own like that. Said as much to Tom apparently. 'Will you put me off at the hospital?' he asked, cool as a cucumber. 'I'm going to see my Grandma.' So that's what he did.'

'But how did he know where to go?'

'Well, he'd been with us enough times to know the direction. In any case, there is only one bus through the town and it stops quite close to the main entrance. The worst he could have done was catch one going in the wrong direction, and that wasn't likely.'

'I'll kill him when I get hold of him,' Guy said.

'Stand in line. I'm his father and I'm first.'

'So how did you find out where he was?'

'That's the most amazing thing of all. He made it to the hospital and found the right ward — God knows how — and when they came round with Mum's supper they just assumed one of us was with him and had gone to the loo. It was only when they did the rounds with the medication and he was still there that they thought to query it.'

'Okay, I grant you have priority, Bas, but I'm definitely second on the list.'

'You will not lay a finger on my son,' said Lucy. 'Actually I think he's been very clever, and he didn't know he was doing anything wrong. I'm proud of him.' With that she burst into tears, but she was smiling through them. They were all smiling.

16

Alexandra had been absent during the crisis. She had of all things gone on a guided tour to Bath, with no great expectation other than the fear she would be mixing with a 'different class of person' as she put it. Like many selfish people she could be charming when she liked, and had struck up an acquaintance with an old army major who'd been sitting next to her on the coach.

'Apparently he lost his wife recently and it's where they used to live. He told me he was taking a trip down memory lane. We spent the whole day together and he knew much more than the guide.'

She spoke with authority, as if the knowledge was her own, unable to resist taking a poke at somebody, but Guy was delighted his mother had enjoyed herself and even more so by the information that they were to meet again. Major Cartwright would be calling ere long. Perhaps they could visit Gloucester next time. With something to focus on, Alexandra became almost pleasant and only managed to put her son's back up three or four times, most particularly when she remarked that Tom needed a good spanking and she hoped he would be punished for his misdemeanour.

'No, Mother, he won't be punished. What he did was potentially dangerous but he did it out of the goodness of his heart.' He paused, wondering if she'd recognise the dig, but there was no reaction. 'If anyone deserves punishment it's me. He was in my charge and I left him to his own devices. I am absolutely mortified.'

'You! Why on earth would you take the blame? I thought it was a bit much, them foisting him on you in the first place.'

'He wasn't foisted on me. I offered.

He's my godson and I should have taken better care of him. I can only be grateful that nothing bad happened, which brings me to the point. I want him under my own roof, and this time I'll take make sure he's properly looked after. Comfortable as it is, a hotel-cum-inn is no place for a five-year-old. I must insist you find somewhere else to stay.'

Alexandra opened her mouth to protest but something in Guy's bearing warned her it would be better not to.

'I can't for the life of me think why you didn't go to a hotel in the first place. You would be pampered, your every whim pandered to.'

'I can't afford a hotel,' she said in what was for her a very small voice. She seemed diminished somehow and for the first time in his life Guy felt sorry for her.

'I am happy to pay for your accommodation, within reason of course, until such time as things are sorted out between you and my father, though I can't understand why you don't have a sufficient allowance.'

'We were extravagant, you see.'

Guy chose to ignore the comment. 'In the meantime you could do worse than concentrate on where you'd like to spend your future. Perhaps a town like Bath, where there is enough of culture to satisfy even you. You'd be far better off in a bustling city than a small town like Rills Ford. Just think of the opportunities it would present you with.'

Guy had spoken with little hope of engaging his mother's interest and was astonished when her eyes lit up with something that looked almost like enthusiasm. He pressed home his advantage. 'If you would prefer, I can lease a cottage for a few months while you decide what to do on a more permanent basis.'

This, it seemed, would not do. Guy could imagine what was going through Alexandra's mind: rubber gloves, washing up, dusting, cooking — things she'd never been keen on and a role which had fallen to Betty in days gone by. On the other hand, in a hotel she would be waited on hand and foot, her bed would be made, food would be presented to her. She'd literally have it on a plate. No contest.

'It would be nice if we could find somewhere with a private sitting room or a suite, as I shall probably be there for some time.'

For Guy there was no contest either. The money he could afford; the presence of his mother he could not abide. 'I'll start browsing the net. Where does this major live? Maybe we could find somewhere close by to enable your outings together.'

'The coach picked him up in the next town.'

Close but not too close, Guy hoped. 'Okay, I'll begin my search there. In the meantime I know you won't like it, but I'm afraid you're going to have to swap with me and Tom.'

Alexandra knew when she was

beaten, and in some strange way was quite proud of the fact that her son had turned out to be such a good adversary. She couldn't resist having the last word though. 'I presume it will be all right for me to leave some of my things here for the time being.'

Guy went off to tell Betty the good news. She was the one person next to himself who had been most affected by Alexandra's presence at the Grange and she did nothing to mask her pleasure when apprised of the situation. The next day Alexandra left and Daisy came home.

* * *

Daisy's return home altered everyone's lives, not the least being her own. Tom, with an abundance of toys to keep him occupied, spent much of each day with his grandmother. *What are godparents for?* was the sentiment both Honey and Guy had expressed when his parents protested they were spoiling him. While

Daisy was never going to be able to return to the Honey Bun to live, not only had she made a remarkable full recovery from the stroke, but her limbs were also healing well. Having relaxed into retirement, as she called it, she found she rather liked being taken care of. The Grange would do very nicely thank you. Without exception they all put her amazing comeback down to her delight in her grandson and the stimulation she received from him; that and her true grit personality.

Honey was dreading the time her brother and his family had to return home, and that time was fast approaching. Would her mother regress? No, she'd come back fighting; it was who she was. Tom couldn't be with her forever and she understood that. Lucy and Basil broke the news of their impending parenthood and though Honey and Guy tried to look surprised, they didn't quite manage to pull it off. Basil raised an eyebrow at his son; just that, no words.

'I couldn't help it, Dad. It just came out, when we were having dinner at the Rose and Crown and the lady on the next table asked if Honey and Guy were having a baby.'

Everyone looked a bit startled but Guy chuckled. 'That's not exactly what happened, and if you can't get your story right, Tom, perhaps you'd better learn to keep your tongue between your teeth.'

'But that would hurt, wouldn't it; biting my tongue?'

Impossible to be cross with him.

'Has anyone noticed what a lovely day it is? I would suggest you get one of the wheelchairs out and take Daisy for a walk,' Betty said, popping into the room during her rounds.

'That's a great idea. It wouldn't do the rest of us any harm either.'

So it was that the group walked into the town. Tom tried to be very helpful as his father pushed the chair, but was persuaded it would be much better for Grandma if he held her hand.

'You know how good you are for her.'

Like anyone else Tom was not averse to a bit of flattery, and spent the rest of the time walking beside rather than behind the wheelchair, a more comfortable arrangement for everyone. Honey was chatting with Lucy, and Guy brought up the rear, as it was impossible to go more than two abreast. From this vantage point he was able to see the whole group and felt more than ever the pull of happy family life, something that had so long eluded him and what he now wanted more than anything else in the world.

Mrs Worthington joined them, coming out of her cottage just as they were walking past, and fell in next to Guy. 'Surely you weren't looking out of your window, were you, Mrs Worthington?' Guy asked with a light in his eye that belied the serious expression on his face.

'As if I would, and don't you be so cheeky, young man. I was just on my way to the teashop for my daily outing.

Is that where you're going?'

It seemed it was, and Honey was delighted to find Suzie in charge when they got there. Basil manoeuvred the wheelchair through the doorway, and chairs were moved inside to accommodate it. Once more the dynamics changed. Daisy, already obviously enjoying the outing, became animated rather than agitated as Honey had feared she might. This had, after all, been her home and her life for so many years. Mrs Worthington sat at the table with her old friend and needed only the odd word from Daisy to maintain a long conversation in which both seemed to take great delight. The rest of the family sat at a different table, leaving room for old acquaintances to join the two ladies. Honey went behind the counter to help Suzie with the sudden influx of people.

'I don't know why I never thought to bring her here before.'

'It could be something to do with an

inability to be in two places at the same time. Remember, you're usually here on your own.'

'Yes, I know, but Henry would have brought her, I'm sure. Look at her, Suzie. I haven't seen her this animated for ages, except when Tom's been with her of course, and he'll be going soon.'

'Well maybe this is just what she needs. Because you haven't done it before doesn't mean you can't in the future.'

'Suzie, I can't tell you how grateful I am to you. To everybody who responded to your article. Why would anyone ever want to live anywhere else?'

'I often ask myself the same question.'

'Lucy told me they'd seen you having dinner with Jack. Don't tell me he's finally seen what's under his nose.'

Suzie went a little pink but did not reply.

'Okay, I'm here when you're ready, but I'm so happy for you.'

'It's early days, Hon, but yes it would

seem he's noticed me at last.'

Honey glanced again at her mother. She was contributing little in the way of conversation; fat chance of getting a word in with Mrs Worthington, but she was totally engaged in it. Suzie followed her friend's gaze.

'Well a change of scenery certainly doesn't seem to have done her any harm. Are you sure it's such a bad idea building a dedicated care home with all the required facilities?'

'Yes, I am! Absolutely sure!'

17

Honey looked across at Guy, sitting with Lucy and Basil, and felt all the old bitterness rise up again. She didn't realise that her anger was in fact at herself, for not thinking before of ways to enrich her mother's life. Maybe the time would come when it wouldn't be possible for Daisy to leave the Grange, and Honey would have to live with that; but the wasted weeks, the time she'd lost, sat heavily upon her conscience. Unwilling or unable to recognise these emotions, she hid them by turning away from herself and towards Guy, whose project she felt sure would further blight her mother's life.

Almost as if he could feel her gaze on him Guy looked up, but instead of the smile he expected to see he was greeted with an icy stare which drove the pleasure from his face. It wasn't too difficult to guess what was upsetting Honey; and Guy, feeling his own guilt still over Tom, was in no mood to sit there and take the blame for something that wasn't his fault. Pushing his chair away from the table, he excused himself to his friends and left the tearooms without a backward glance. Outside he looked first right and then left, frustration holding him motionless, until he turned right, away from the direction they'd all come earlier, and marched along at a hell of a pace. It was exhilarating, or would have been if he hadn't been too worked up to enjoy it. By the time he'd taken a couple of turns and his pace had slowed somewhat, he'd reached the home of an ally — Mary Simpson. Without hesitation he turned in at the gate and was welcomed by his old teacher.

'Whatever is the matter, Guy? You look as if something awful has happened.'

Guy poured everything into her willing ears: the dread he'd felt when

Tom had gone missing; the guilt after he'd been found. From there he went on to describe the day's outing which for him had ended with the look of (he said) hate in Honey's face that had sent him rushing headlong from the place.

'She's still dead set against it, is she?'

'More than ever, I think.'

'And still she hasn't seen the plans.'

'To do her justice, Mary, I don't think it would matter if the plans were perfect, which they pretty much are as it happens. It's the idea of moving Daisy at all that she can't or won't come to terms with.'

'She's frightened, Guy. You can understand that surely.'

'I do, and in her case and that of the other residents' families there may be some justification. It's the rest I'm mad at, the people who've condemned the scheme out of hand without even knowing what it is.'

'That's a small town for you. In fact, that's human nature — for some people anyway. There will always be those who look for trouble. How are things going anyway, with the plans?'

'I haven't had consent through yet, but I have been told that in principle they can't see why there should be any problem. To be honest I can't wait to get started. Usually my job is finished when I submit the plans, but this time I'll be seeing the project right through to the end.'

'And you're excited about it, Guy. I can see that much.'

'A little bit of me wants to prove them all wrong but mostly it's . . . I know this is going to sound soft . . . mostly it's because I want to help people. The care home issue is an emotional one and so many of them are not up to scratch, due either to staff or facilities. As you well know I'm not all that fond of my mother but I wouldn't want to see her end up in a place that's run on old-fashioned institutional lines, which still happens in some places, believe me, or managed by people who cut corners because they have to make it pay. I understand it has to be about profit and loss to a certain extent but that's not going to be an issue in The New Grange. I want my people to be happy in their old age.'

'You're a good man, Guy, and I know you have a battle on your hands but at the end of the day, barring refusal of planning consent, you will get your way and realise your dream.'

'Why can't she see that?'

He didn't have to mention Honey's name. Mary Simpson wasn't stupid.

* * *

A week later Lucy and Basil returned to Australia, taking Tom with them. The difference in Daisy was apparent almost immediately and though everyone concerned knew how good her grandson had been for her none of them had expected quite such a strong reaction now he was gone. She soon pulled herself together though, pragmatic as ever, and it seemed she was already

195

planning a visit to Australia at Christmas in time to welcome her new grandchild into the world. Realistic or not it gave her something to focus on. Honey, tied down more to the shop now her mother was no longer in hospital, did her best and on the occasions she was able to take Daisy out in the wheelchair there was talk of nothing but the proposed adventure. Mrs Worthington went to visit her old friend on an almost daily basis and Betty watched as the pile of holiday brochures grew and grew.

*   *   *

The petition Suzie had worked so hard on had been presented to the Planning Committee and had been rejected. Those in the know were well aware that the Grange in its present state would lose its licence at the next time of renewal and were keen to get the project off the ground. In fact, if it weren't for the submission of the current plans, the Grange's role as a care home would have been terminated at the next council meeting . . . and amazingly still nobody had asked to see the plans. Permission was granted and work began almost immediately. Guy and Honey hardly saw each other in the next few weeks, and any talk of starting a patisserie joint venture had fallen by the wayside. While the foundations were being dug Guy left Rills Ford. He hadn't told anybody he was going or what he was doing except Betty, and she wasn't about to betray his confidence. In fact he'd gone to France to see his father. While Guy was in a position to support his mother, and to get her out of his hair was willing to do so, he couldn't believe his father had left her without any means of support, tempted though he might have been. He wanted to find out what the real situation was.

* * *

Back in Rills Ford, Honey didn't know whether to be relieved or angry. After fourteen years away Guy had returned and filled her life, bringing back all the old feelings she'd had for him and setting her in turmoil. No longer a doting teenager, it was fairly obvious to her that there was an attraction on both sides now, though neither of them had said anything. But it seemed the Fates were against them and, as she couldn't reconcile herself to what he was planning to do at the Grange, neither could she reconcile herself to what to her seemed his high-handed attitude. In a way it was a relief not to look up every time the door opened in the hope or expectation of seeing him, but all of a sudden she felt lonely and alone. Impotent to do anything about the new care home, her anger bubbled away just below the surface, and it was a brave person indeed who tried to talk to her about it.

* * *

198

Suzie, too, was upset at the outcome of the petition, because she'd been genuinely concerned for the reasons she'd given at the time. However, after one of the councillors, a friend of hers, dropped a small hint in her ear, she finally visited the planning office to see for herself. Mortified at the realisation that she'd unjustifiably been so much of a pain in Guy's side, she was sorrier still not to be able to apologise in person now he'd left the district. Though it hurt her to do so, she put a front page retraction (with Jack's permission) in the *Rills Ford Post* and an apology for stirring the waters. The fact that she'd been wrong did her no harm in anyone's eyes; that she had the honesty to admit it openly did her a lot of good. There weren't many people who thought very highly about those in the newspaper business and such frankness was refreshing. It wasn't something she could discuss with Honey, though, whose reasons for not wanting the new build remained the same and who remained unaware that the Grange in its present state was already condemned.

Powerless to help her friend, Suzie was consoled by her blossoming relationship with Jack. All her dreams were coming true and though the lengthening of the days heralded spring, she felt as if it was Christmas or New Year. Jack, who had seemed unaware of her existence except as an employee, had become so attentive that things were moving almost faster than she was comfortable with, but she was prepared to go with the flow; and where Honey looked strained and pale, Suzie was flushed and vibrant. A Rills Fordian to her fingertips, she was establishing a reputation for herself in her home town, and at last it seemed her love life was taking off too.

18

It had been three years since Guy had last been to France to visit his parents, and the change in his father was astonishing. Not that he'd aged! If anything he looked ten years younger, and when Guy was introduced to the reason for this remarkable transformation it was easy to see why. Candice was about forty-five years old, several years his father's junior but a woman with the ability to make anyone she met feel vibrant and alive. There was a sparkle about her you couldn't help but respond to, and for Edward Ffoulkes it was as though he'd been given a new lease of life. Suspicious at first, Guy had reacted to Candice in the same way as most other people she met. He decided very quickly she wasn't after his father's money; in fact she was wealthier than him in her own right. That she valued the nobility of his ancestry was in no doubt; she admitted as much at their first meeting.

'He told me he had relatives fighting at the Battle of Agincourt. On the wrong side, *malheureusement*, but to have such history!'

She seemed a bit in awe and Guy wasn't at all sure his father hadn't exaggerated slightly about his antecedents — but who was he to interfere? In any case, it might have been true. That Candice idolised Edward couldn't have been more obvious if she'd worn a sign around her neck, and Guy had to remind himself that his father was only in his early sixties. Living with Alexandra had made him appear much older. As to Candice, Guy couldn't believe it was anything other than a meeting of hearts and souls for both of them. It was out of character, though, for him not to have provided for Alexandra; and whereas Guy had come expecting Candice to have been the cause, he ruled that out almost immediately. A more generous-hearted person one couldn't hope to meet, and she had no reason to deprive Edward's wife, other than resentment for the life she'd led with him. Not managing to get his father alone until the day after his arrival, he asked the question immediately when the opportunity presented itself.

'It's not like you, Dad, to leave Mother on the breadline. What happened, anyway? Is it something you want to talk about?'

Edward it seemed was ready to talk for as long as his son wanted to listen. 'Candice is adorable. I can't imagine how I spent so long under your mother's thumb. I haven't enjoyed myself so much in years, if ever . . . On the breadline? Candice wants me to do the right thing.'

Guy interrupted here, not sure whether the suggested 'right thing' was to divorce his mother and marry Candice or what.

'Good Lord, no. Candice doesn't

want to get married. She's quite happy the way things are. No, she was adamant I make your mother — ' It was as if he couldn't even speak her name. ' — a generous allowance.'

'So why didn't you?'

That pulled Edward up short. 'Is that what she told you? That I didn't provide for her?'

Guy flushed slightly, angry that he'd been taken in so easily, and more so because he should have known better. 'No, in fact she told me when she arrived that you'd promised her liberal support, but then she said she wanted to stay at the Grange and gave me the impression, probably intentionally, that she was strapped for cash.'

'Almost certainly intentionally. And did you allow her to stay at the Grange?'

Guy looked as sheepish as it was possible for a man of his size to do. 'I did at first. You know how difficult she can be.'

'None better.'

'Well she's not there now, thank goodness, and I think in fairness she'd rather have a place of her own.' Guy looked at his father and, raising an eyebrow, said, 'I think she was lonely at first.'

Edward spluttered in the act of sipping his drink.

'Quite, but it was true. You'll never believe it. She actually went on a coach outing to Bath. With the common people!'

'You're kidding me.'

By this time both men were thoroughly amused, but the gem was when Guy dropped the next piece of information. 'No, and she's found a man friend.'

'You're kidding me,' Edward repeated, reaching for and collapsing into a chair like a man who was too overcome to support himself.

'A widower, and he seems to have taken a fancy to Mother. He is apparently quite happy to be her escort, and he's a retired army major so that suits her sense of status well enough.

I'm hoping to find her a cottage close to where he lives and that's really why I've come to see you.'

'She doesn't need my permission to buy a cottage and she knows full well the funds will be available to her.'

'I was beginning to think I was going to have to provide the funding myself.'

Edward bridled a little. 'I may not be able to live with the woman anymore, but I will at least make sure she is comfortably accommodated.'

'Okay, you can come down off your high horse.' He paused for a moment. 'It seems I've made the journey for nothing then.'

'I hope you don't feel that way. I'm always delighted to see you, my boy, and I'm glad you've met Candice. No matter what I might have told you, or your mother for that matter, there's nothing like forming your own opinion.'

'She's delightful. I may even try to steal her away from you.'

'No chance. She likes older men.'

'It would seem you're not as old as I

thought you were!'

'Me neither — and getting younger every day.'

* * *

Guy was in no hurry to return to Rills Ford. Seeing Honey nearly every day and never knowing from one to the next how he was going to be received was torture for him. Not that he blamed her. Unlike many of the town's residents, she at least had a good personal reason for her protestations, but he knew that in her mind he was the bad guy (with a small g) who was causing upheaval to her mother's life. He had no guarantee, either, that Daisy or indeed any of the other residents would not take a downturn when the time came to move them. That the move was inevitable was irrelevant; Honey would blame him. Unable to see a way forward and unwilling to undergo unnecessary torment, he decided to accept the invitation to spend a couple of weeks at his father's villa. The time would come when he'd have to return to oversee his project, but while the groundwork was being done he had no need to be in England.

'Why don't you two go and have a round of golf, eh? I am having a tennis lesson with the new coach. Not that I need lessons, of course, but he is *magnifique* and only twenty-eight. Do you think I might attach him to me?'

'If it makes you happy, my darling, attach him by all means. I'll just stay and chat up the receptionist at the club; give you a bit more time together.'

It was obvious to Guy that this sort of banter went on all the time and even more obvious that the two were totally in love. He couldn't help feeling just a tiny bit envious. He and Edward caught up with the players on the third tee and stood back to wait.

'You say Candice doesn't want to marry you?'

'That's right.'

'Do you know why?'

'Her husband and son drowned in a boating accident. I think she doesn't want to be tied to anyone in that way again.'

'But you're devoted to each other. That much is plain for all the world to see.'

'And as such neither of us has the need for a ring. She's a woman. She's French. She's superstitious. Any one of those would be enough for me not to try and persuade her. In any case, at our age, does it really matter? What about you? I'd have thought our marriage, your mother's and mine, would have been enough to put you off for life. No special somebody waiting for you in Australia or Hong Kong?'

Guy loved his father and trusted him implicitly. He also admired the courage it had taken to split with Alexandra and he had a newfound respect for the man he used to believe was weak. He wasn't ready yet, though, to confide in anyone about his feelings for Honey. Mary had made it obvious that she knew and he was pretty certain Betty did as well, and even probably Mrs Worthington. He was confident his secret was safe with them.

'No, nobody. You're probably right. I didn't have the greatest example, did I?'

'Don't let it blight your future, son, and don't make the same mistakes I did. What you need is a woman with a strong personality who you can have fun with.' Guy knew he was talking about Candice. 'Not one who wants to dominate you.' And no prizes for guessing who that was either.

Guy knew he could have fun with Honey. On the rare occasions she allowed her obligations to take a back seat, she was an absolute joy to be with, possessing a wicked sense of humour that matched his own. No, it was circumstances that were threatening to make a middle-aged woman of the thirty-year-old with a sense of the ridiculous that so much appealed to him. And instead of lightening that load it seemed he was just increasing the weight of it. Not knowing how to solve the problem and not wanting to exacerbate it, Guy stayed away.

He contrived to have a pretty good time as well. Unaware of his commitment to Honey, Candice did everything she could to throw him in the way of some of the beautiful young women who came within her circle. Guy fell into old habits, charming them without making any fall in love with him. He made it plain he was unavailable and once the ground rules were established, he spent the next two weeks at sport and play, dining lavishly at some of the many restaurants available and having a thoroughly good time. He was almost sorry when the time came for him to leave. The project at the Grange was moving on and his presence was required. That was what he told himself, but regardless of the fun he'd been having thoughts of Honey increasingly occupied him; and in spite of the torment he knew he would suffer, he couldn't wait to get back to her.

19

Honey felt as if a light had gone out in her life. The brother she adored, together with his wife and their son, had returned to Australia, leaving a void she was finding it difficult to cope with. They say you don't miss what you've never had, but in Lucy she'd found a friend and in Tom a feeling she couldn't even begin to put into words. Now another niece or nephew was on the way, and heaven alone knew how long it would be before that new acquaintance was made. If her mother had her way Daisy would see them before Honey, who could see no way of leaving the business to travel abroad.

Circumstances had put Honey in the tearooms and up until now she hadn't questioned her situation; after all, she truly loved what she did for a living. She'd never thought of a different future — one with a family, with children of her own. But she was thinking of it now. Before, she'd had no experience of what it could be like. Basil's visit had changed that. Before, the only man she would ever even have considered in the role of soulmate was travelling the world, enjoying other women, thinking of her — if indeed he ever did think of her — only as a scrubby kid.

But he'd come back into her life as well, and changed everything. And now he'd gone again. Had been gone for almost two weeks, and she had no idea when or even if he would return. And if he did? There was no understanding between them and a good deal of animosity on her side, which was a barrier to the feelings she tried so hard to suppress. And where did that animosity come from? She needed no reminder that work was proceeding at the Grange in its owner's absence. Whether Guy came back or not, the new care home would be built. Her mother would have to move; her mother, who somehow didn't regard the impending change with the same dread as her daughter. *She just doesn't know how difficult it might be.*

With her usual practicality Honey got on with the job, did what she could to make her mother's life a little brighter, and gave no indication to the outside world how unhappy she really was. *I'm damned if I'll let anyone see me cry.* But cry she did, in the privacy of her room, late at night, when for a few hours she could allow the mask to drop; could admit to herself how much she was missing Guy; how much she dreaded his return and how lonely she was without him. Always the final thing she saw before falling into fitful sleep was the shock on his face a couple of weeks before he'd left, a look she had herself induced. She could still hear the scrape of the chair as he hurriedly pushed it back from the table and rushed out of the Honey Bun without so much as a backward glance.

* * *

'Oops! Sorry. My fault. In too much of a hurry as usual.'

Honey found herself clasped firmly by her upper arms, which was just as well or she'd have fallen over. She'd almost been felled by the man who was now smiling ruefully at her as he stepped back to allow her into the Grange.

'I've come to see my dad. He moved in a couple of days ago. We were lucky to get the place. Been on the waiting list for ages.'

As he paused for breath Honey took the opportunity to introduce herself and Betty, who had joined them. 'I expect we'll be seeing a bit of each other then. My mother's here too. I'm Honey Bunting and this is Betty, the manager.'

'Rufus. Rufus Thornberry. I'll be back in a minute. Got to get something from the car. See you inside.' With that he was off, and Honey felt as if she'd encountered a whirlwind. Once inside she stopped to talk to Betty in the foyer, when the door opened and her new acquaintance came back in, only this time he was not alone. Looking at her with huge round brown eyes was a golden retriever, straining towards her but held firmly by his lead. He obviously wanted to be her friend.

'Is it okay if I stroke him?' she asked as she moved towards the dog, but before his owner had time to answer he rolled over, offering her his tummy. Honey lost her heart to him. She wasn't the first and she wouldn't be the last. Rufus laughed.

'Up to your tricks again, eh, Ruff?' he said to his dog. And then to her: 'Ruff by name but definitely not by nature. Silly, I know, but well ... Ruff and Rufus, Rufus and Ruff. One man and his dog. Like I said — silly.'

Honey didn't think it was silly at all and decided she'd like to get to know both her new acquaintances rather better.

'Come in, Rufus,' said Betty. 'It's a wonderful idea and I don't know why we never thought of it before. You've heard of the PAT dog scheme, Honey? Pets as Therapy. Apparently Rufus and Ruff are regular visitors to the hospital.'

Honey looked at Rufus with respect. Anyone who gave their time to help others was okay in her book.

'It wasn't until Derek arrived and we got talking that the subject ever came up,' Betty added. 'Derek is in Room Five now that poor Mr Gable has had to go into hospice care.'

'And I'm sorry of course about Mr Gable, but so glad we've got Dad in here at last. He's been waiting a long time and we were beginning to despair and think he might have to go elsewhere. It was a close-run thing. He hasn't been managing at home for a long time now.'

Honey wondered if Rufus knew there was to be further upheaval when the new home was built. Apparently he did, she found out later, and he was quite sanguine about it. 'With the care that Betty and her staff give and in such beautiful surroundings, it has to be streets better than some of the places I've seen,' she said.

They were in the foyer once again, each on their way out after Honey had spent time with Daisy, and Rufus and Ruff had introduced themselves to the residents, most of whom were sitting in the lounge, so Honey was able to see their immediate response. Faces lit up; arthritic hands that could barely move managed to pat the dog's head or stroke his back. Daisy, too, seemed delighted, and certainly the change in atmosphere in the room was tangible.

'Will you be here again tomorrow?'

'Unfortunately, no. I live some distance away and I'll only be able to get here a couple of times a week. But even though I won't see as much of Dad, I'm happier to have him being looked after twenty-four hours a day rather than being left on his own while I'm at work.'

'He lives with you? Lived with you?'

'Yes, but I travel a lot and Ruff often comes with me. I used to leave him at home sometimes — you know, to keep Dad company — but mostly he came with me. I suppose it sounds selfish but that's why I got him in the first place. I spend hours in the car and it keeps my blood pressure levels down just having him sitting next to me. It's what made me think of offering him as a PAT dog. You've no idea how calming the presence of a dog can be.'

'I saw the evidence just now. Well, I hope to see you again soon, Rufus. It's been nice meeting you.'

'Do you always come at this time?'

'Usually.'

'Then I shall make a point of doing the same. It's been nice meeting you too, Honey.' And there was no doubting the warmth in those words.

* * *

Honey's spirits were lifted as much as those of the residents of the Grove. While baking later that evening she realised she was humming to herself. Other than Guy — and she didn't want to think about Guy — it had been a long time since anyone had shown any interest in her. *Opportunity would be a fine thing*. But opportunity had presented itself without her going in search of it. That Rufus was attracted to her was without question. She was astute and honest enough to acknowledge that. Would he take it any further? Only time would tell. In the meantime it was nice to realise that for some, at least, she was a desirable young woman.

Even in her private moments she'd never given much thought to herself. Some safety mechanism had prevented her going down a path she couldn't follow because of other commitments. Her mother and her work had been her life. Now, in a few short weeks, two men had entered her domain and her perspective was changing. Of Guy she had no hopes, but if Rufus chose to ask her out she would definitely go. She'd enjoyed his company enormously in the short time she'd spent with him — and was still feeling as if she'd encountered a whirlwind!

20

By the time Guy returned just over a
week later, Honey had already been on
her second date with Rufus and was
enjoying a social life she hadn't realised
she'd missed. On Sunday Rufus took
her for a drive in the country, stopping
for lunch at what he said was one of his
favourite pubs. The days were warm
enough now — as long as one wore a
sweater — for sitting outside, and Ruff
lay quietly at their feet under the table
in the garden.

'I can hardly move, I've eaten so
much,' Honey said as she pushed her
plate away.

'Time to get going then. There's a
circular walk.' The word 'walk' was a
catalyst that had Ruff on his feet and
bouncing around with excitement.
'Okay, boy, in a minute,' Rufus said,
stroking his head. 'There's a circular

walk from across the road, so we can leave the car here. Did you remember to bring your walking shoes?'

'After you reminded me twice, how could I forget?' Honey answered, smiling at him.

'Well it's a nice day now, but we've had a fair bit of rain and it can be quite mucky out there, as I'm sure Ruff will give the truth to by the time we get back. I don't want you turning an ankle on me.'

This of course reminded Honey of her outing with Guy, but she put it resolutely to the back of her mind.

'They're in the bag, the one I put in the back of the car before we left.'

'Right, let's go for it then.'

* * *

Once off the road and onto the footpath, Ruff was released from his restraint and disappeared quickly into the distance. He had work to do. Not forgetting his manners, he kept returning to check on his humans before rushing off again to explore his world.

'A golden dog with a long coat who loves water. You made a good choice there,' Honey said wryly when Ruff stood patiently being rubbed down at the end of their walk.

'Yes, I don't suppose there was a puddle he didn't roll in. Look at him though. Did you ever see such a picture of happiness?'

'No, nor smell such a whiffy one,' she replied as Ruff settled on the blanket which covered the back seat.

'Don't be so proper. Didn't you like to get yourself mucky when you were a kid?'

'Loved it. Has it ever occurred to you this kid isn't going to grow up?'

'Nor would I want him to. I know one thing. If there's another life after this one I'm coming back as a dog.'

★　★　★

The next time she went out with Rufus was after they'd both been visiting their respective parents.

'I shouldn't really. I've still got my baking to do.'

'Just a quick meal, then, and I'll have you home in no time. Ruff is fine in the car for a while. It's his second home. Come on, Honey. You've got to eat.'

The Rose and Crown was busy by the time they got there but they managed to find a table. It was near the door and there was a bit of a draught, but it was that or nothing, and they weren't going to let it spoil their evening. It seemed as if the world and his wife came in that evening, if not to eat then to have a drink, and there were a few raised eyebrows. People weren't used to seeing Honey out enjoying herself and several wondered who this stranger was.

They were at the coffee stage when Suzie and Jack walked in, so after the initial introductions they all adjourned to the bar. Jack and Rufus hit it off immediately and during their conversation Honey discovered Rufus, who hadn't told her much about himself, was the area manager for a national company trading in components — of what, she didn't know — and this was the reason for him spending a lot of time on the road.

'He's obviously staked his claim,' Honey whispered to Suzie, referring to Jack sitting with his arm around her best friend's shoulders.

'I can't believe it. I've waited so long and now it's perfect. Do you really think he feels the same?'

'Actually I think it's rather nice. It's not like he's being possessive, which I know you'd hate. It's more that he's comfortable in this relationship.'

Suzie smiled contentedly and everybody relaxed into the evening. Rufus slipped out once to check on Ruff, and nobody was more astonished than Honey when the landlord called closing time.

After one glass of wine at dinner

Rufus had stuck to water, but Honey was way above her normal maximum and staggered slightly when the cold night air hit her as he escorted her across the road.

'Watch out! I didn't insist on walking shoes the other day to have you break a leg this evening. Will you be okay? You're surely not going to start baking now?'

Honey looked at her watch, though she knew what the time was because of the Rose and Crown's opening hours.

'I've done it before.'

'Not in this state surely?'

'Probably not, but I need to have something to offer my customers tomorrow.'

'All right. Tell you what I'll do. I'll take Ruff round the block a couple of times and come back. If you still want to go ahead I'll come in and give you a hand.'

'You bake?'

'You eat?'

Honey had never worked in the

kitchen with anyone other than her mother before, but she found it companionable and also discovered that Rufus could take instruction and was happy to help in whatever way he could. At two o'clock they had a cup of coffee and he left, kissing her tenderly on the cheek. Sober by now, Honey had plenty of time to analyse whether or not she'd enjoyed it. She found she wanted to repeat the experience. *Just to check. After all, it was so quick I didn't really have a chance to appreciate it.* She was just on the point of falling asleep when her phone signalled a text message.

'Thank you for a lovely evening. Can we do it again soon? Sleep well.'

Honey passed a dreamless night and woke feeling a lot better than she deserved.

★   ★   ★

The evenings were lighter now, at the time both Honey and Rufus visited their parents, and Rufus was interested enough in the new development to ask Honey to go and look at it with him. She agreed grudgingly, and they walked through the grounds to see what was going on. Access by road would be out of the question for some time, the plans being that a slip road off the main driveway to the Grange would be laid to the new buildings. In the meantime gravel had been put down not so much to protect the grass — it would be covered by tarmac later anyway — but as a damage limitation exercise to prevent the builders' vehicles going further afield than was necessary.

There was little to see when they got there. The site had been excavated and the foundations put down, but there was no identifiable structure yet. Even so, it was impressive.

'It looks huge, doesn't it? Do you know how many rooms it's going to have?' Rufus asked Honey.

'I haven't been to look at the plans. I'm not really interested.'

'But your mother will be living here.

There's nothing you can do about that.'
Honey had made him well aware of her
feelings about the whole thing. 'Don't
you want to know what it's going to be
like?'

'I don't want her to move at all.'

Rufus turned Honey towards him, his
face full of concern. 'You've made that
abundantly clear, but have you ever
wondered how Guy might feel? It's not
just his home, it's his ancestral home.
How do you think you'd feel in his
position?'

Honey had never even looked at it
from Guy's point of view. She'd just
thought he was being selfish and
high-handed, but Rufus had put the
whole thing into a different perspective.
Perhaps in her anxiety for Daisy she
hadn't been able to see anything else. It
didn't alter the situation, that she was
convinced a move would be harmful to
her mother, but it did at least make her
think she was perhaps a bit unreasonable in her condemnation of Guy. And
now he was gone and she might never

have the chance to apologise. She shivered.

'You're cold. Come on, let's get you back inside.'

She allowed Rufus to lead her back to the Grange, but suddenly all the pleasure she'd gained out of the past few weeks seemed to disappear into the evening air. Guy had once more filled her mind and she didn't like it. She didn't like it at all.

They went back into the building for a short time, just for one last check on Daisy and Derek, after which Rufus insisted on giving Honey a lift home. She'd quite have enjoyed the walk. It would have given her the opportunity to assimilate this new information, or at least this new take on the information she already had. It seemed churlish, though, to refuse.

As they pulled out of the drive they were passed by Guy's beautiful car. Honey's heart leapt into her throat. *He's back! He's come back.* To Rufus it was just another car. He'd never met

231

Guy and didn't know what vehicle he drove. For his part Guy didn't give them a second glance. He was glad to be home. Glad and anxious. How would Honey receive him? They had parted on bad terms. Hadn't parted at all in fact. He'd just walked out. Perhaps it was just as well he didn't know he'd almost rubbed shoulders with her in the company of another man.

21

It didn't take Guy long to discover Honey was seeing someone else.

'You've just missed Honey and Rufus,' Betty said as he came through the door, forgetting he'd never met the other man. 'I saw them walking over to the new development so maybe he'll be able to knock some sense into her. She seems to listen to what he says.'

'Rufus?'

'Oh of course; he wasn't here when you went away, was he? His father has moved in to Mr Gable's old room. He brings his dog in when he comes to visit. Ruff, a golden retriever. He's a PAT dog.'

'A what?' Guy had never come across the expression before.

'It's when people take their dogs to visit patients in hospitals or homes; even their own homes, I think. It stands for Pets as Therapy and is supposed to be very calming, and to help when people are missing their own pet. He's done wonders for the residents here.'

'Sounds like a great scheme. It's good of him to give up his time.'

'I think he's pleased to do it. Evidently he does hospital visiting as well.'

Betty hesitated, not quite sure how to break the news of Rufus and Honey's developing relationship. She could only guess how Guy felt about her, and he was a man whose feelings ran deep. Straightforward was the only way, she decided. Better to find out from her than one of the town gossips. She lowered her voice slightly as people do when imparting bad news.

'They've been seeing each other.'

Betty could almost see the veil come down over Guy's face; could feel the tenseness in his body. Her heart ached for him, the lonely boy who had become a lonely man. He looked defeated.

'It's only been a couple of times. Nothing serious, I don't think,' Betty added, trying to soften the blow.

'I suppose it was inevitable she would meet someone soon, a beautiful woman like that. Ah well, it's none of my business, I suppose.' He smiled wanly at Betty. 'It was obvious she was never going to be interested in me.'

To Betty nothing was less obvious, but now wasn't the time to tell him; and anyway, she didn't think she ought to interfere. She changed the subject. 'So you managed to avoid being snapped up by one of Candice's friends.'

'My heart wasn't in it.'

She left him to unpack.

* * *

Guy stood still in his room, not sure what to do next. While he hadn't held out much hope of his prospects, this had nevertheless been a real body blow. He looked at his case lying on the bed, still unopened.

I could just turn round and go straight back. Maybe if I distance myself it won't hurt so much.

But Guy wasn't a quitter and he had a project to see through to completion, something he couldn't or didn't want to do from a distance. Also, though he couldn't have Honey, he still wanted to retain her friendship. *If all she can do is see me as Basil's best mate, then that's how it will have to be.* Consequently, the next time he saw her it was to apologise for leaving so abruptly and not saying where he was going.

'I needed to see my father, to find out what arrangements he'd made for my mother before I start looking for somewhere for her to live.'

They were standing in the foyer at the Grange and it wasn't one of the days Rufus visited, so Guy knew they were free from interruption. Honey had been nervous about seeing him again but he made it easy for her. Switching on the charm was second nature to him

— it was a tool he'd practised and honed over the years by way of self-preservation — and she followed his lead, but to her he'd never seemed further away. She smiled somewhat ruefully, whether because of her own circumstances or because of his mother even she couldn't be sure.

'And how is Edward? I haven't seen him for years.'

'Twenty years younger, or at least that's what he looks like. I can't imagine what it must have been like living with such a cold fish for so long.'

'Your mother was certainly not in the habit of engaging with anyone as far as I remember.'

'Engaging is the last word I'd use to describe her. Candice couldn't be more different if she tried — but that's what I liked so much about her. She doesn't try. She's quite naturally warm and loving and absolutely dotty about my father.'

Honey and Guy had been friends for long enough for her to ask without embarrassment, 'And how do you plan to deal with Alexandra?'

'I'm hoping she's taken enough with Major Cartwright to move to Bens Ford. That's where he lives.'

'Major Cartwright?'

'Didn't I tell you? She's found herself a beau. Retired army major and a widower. Seems he taken quite a shine to her.'

'She must have been trying really hard.'

They both laughed, and all the more so when he told her about the coach outing.

'Your mother!'

'You'd better believe it.'

'So you think it'll work, her moving to Bens Ford? I can't picture her standing at the kitchen sink wearing her Marigolds.'

'It's funny, that's exactly what I thought. But maybe — and I realise I'm stretching it a bit here — she's been spoilt. My father must have seen something in her all those years ago.

Perhaps he's partly to blame.'

'Just don't let go of that elastic band while you're stretching. It'll hit you right in the face. Guy, she was never a warm person.'

'No, but she may well have been a disappointed one. My father told me she always wanted a daughter. I'm not sure if he meant as a second child or instead of me; the latter, I shouldn't be at all surprised.'

'You're being too hard on yourself. Anyway, I still can't picture her in a cottage.'

'Neither could I at first, but just think — if she employs a gardener and someone to do the housework, she'll be living exactly the kind of life she likes. Drastically scaled down, of course, but still lady of her own small manor.'

'And how do you go about finding this small manor?'

'I did some searching online while I was in France. There are a couple up for sale at the moment. In fact I'm taking her to see them now.'

Honey watched him leave. Both had regrets. Neither knew about the other.

★ ★ ★

As it turned out, Alexandra didn't like either of the properties on offer but she was very taken with Bens Ford itself. All the more so when Guy took her to one of the local restaurants for dinner to find Major Cartwright seated alone at one of the tables. Guy was astonished at the change in his parent. While she didn't go so far as to simper she certainly became almost little girlish, and definitely much softer around the edges. The major waved at them, standing with old-fashioned propriety as he did so, and introductions were made. Mother and son were invited to join the table.

'There I was, feeling like a lonely old man, and a ray of sunshine walked in.'

Guy thought this a bit over the top until he saw Alexandra's reaction. He felt as if he'd never met her before

— and indeed in this guise he hadn't. His mother's beau stood behind Alexandra and pushed in her chair as she sat down. *Old-world manners which will suit my mother very well.* Guy's role for the rest of the evening was little more than that of observer, though Winston — the major — tried to engage him in conversation. Not so Guy's mother. Her son was delighted to see the major was no pushover, and that his mother responded well to being gently reprimanded on the two occasions she spoke out of turn. *This will do. Definitely this will do. Maybe if my father . . .* Guy took the thought no further. Edward was happy with Candice and if Alexandra could find happiness with Winston, then so be it.

'I see you're looking at your watch, dear boy.' Guy took no exception to the epithet. 'If time is pressing, I would be delighted to drive your mother home when we've finished our digestif.'

Guy realised he was de trop and took his leave, shaking hands formally and with much gusto with the major and enjoying it far more than the obligatory peck on his mother's cheek. Reflecting on an evening that was far more enjoyable than he'd expected, he was still smiling ten minutes later when he drove past the Honey Bun — and such a feeling of loss descended on him that he felt almost unable to finish his journey.

★ ★ ★

Honey had had a pleasant enough evening as well, double-dating with Suzie and Jack. Resolutely putting Guy out of her mind — an impossible task, but she awarded herself at least an E for effort — Honey tried to concentrate on her companions. The clocks had sprung forward and the longer days had, it seemed, lightened everyone's mood.

'Ruff enjoys his walks so much more in daylight. I'd have thought his nose would have been enough but it seems that he, like the rest of us, is grateful for the arrival of spring.'

'Where is he tonight?' Jack asked.

For a moment Rufus looked slightly disconcerted before replying, 'Oh, I've left him at home. He'll be okay.'

'Isn't it rather a long time to leave him,' Suzie wondered, 'taking into account your travelling time and all?'

'He'll sleep right through after the walk he had before I came out. No, he'll be fine.'

Rufus had recovered his equilibrium but the others were puzzled to know what had disturbed him. All were too polite or felt they didn't know him well enough to ask. Unusually, though, he didn't linger at the end of the evening, excusing himself while they were still drinking their coffee, and saying, 'I hope you'll forgive me if I don't stop. After what you said I'm feeling guilty about Ruff.' Turning to Honey he added, 'I'll phone you tomorrow if that's okay.'

They all looked at each other after

he'd left. 'Have I just been given the brush-off or what?' Honey commented.

'I think it's 'or what', but I'd love to know what the 'or what' is.'

'So would I, Suzie. So would I.'

22

Honey didn't lose any sleep over Rufus. The only emotion she experienced was curiosity. If she'd thought his affections were engaged she'd have ended their relationship; she wasn't dishonest enough to continue when her heart wasn't in it. There was no doubt he was attracted to her, but it seemed almost as if he was enjoying the companionship without wanting any more, much as she was. Although he'd kissed her a few times, there was little passion involved on either side. Honey had been happy to continue in this way, enjoying getting out and doing things after Guy had made her realise how limited her life was. Guy. Always it came back to Guy. *Fifteen years or more is a long time to carry a torch for someone who only regards me in the light of a younger sister.*

The next time Rufus called, he acted as if nothing had happened and asked if she could join him and Ruff for a walk on Sunday afternoon after they'd visited their parents. Honey was glad he hadn't waited until a chance meeting at the Grange and was surprised to discover that she was looking forward to the outing. Spring had awoken in her a dissatisfaction with her mundane existence (she'd never seen it that way before) and a desire to get out and do things. Spring? Rufus? Guy? What or whoever was the cause, she was ready to take her life in her hands and *do* something.

★ ★ ★

At the Grange Honey found Derek Thornberry sitting with her mother. Rufus was nowhere to be seen, but she was a bit early.

'Hello, Derek. How are you?'

'Enjoying a natter with Daisy here. And you?'

It seemed he and Daisy had struck up a friendship, and Derek obviously enjoyed putting people at their ease as much as his son. His residence in the care home was one of physical necessity not mental incapacity, and as long as he could find someone to wheel him around he was happy to give his time to anyone who needed him or wanted a bit of company. He asked Honey to find one of the carers so he could leave her alone with Daisy. He didn't say as much, but it was obvious to Honey and she admired his tact.

Daisy seemed quite bright, so maybe Derek had worked a little magic. She took her mother out into the afternoon sunshine and pushed her around the enclosed garden that had been sectioned off for the exclusive use of the home. The garden, any garden, had always been Daisy's passion — witness the naming of her children — and in early April the daffodils were spreading sunshine all over the place. The tulips weren't open yet and in their present state they had always reminded Honey of paintbrushes, standing as they did on upright stems and with their yet-to-unfold flowers looking like thick sable brushes that had just been dipped in oil ready for the canvas. Daisy beamed as they passed a bright red camellia, sitting beside a smallish magnolia. With her good hand she pointed excitedly at the base of the tree where bluebells, unready but determined, had forced their way through the earth into daylight.

'Look at the bluebells, Honey!'

Honey knelt down in front of her mother and took both hands in hers. 'Yes, Mum, they're beautiful.'

Impossible to tell if Daisy saw the tears in Honey's eyes, but they flowed unashamedly when they reached the bottom of the garden and Daisy pointed again. 'Honeysuckle!'

It was indeed honeysuckle; not yet in flower, but advanced enough for an expert to identify it — and Daisy was an expert. The delight on her face was still apparent when they returned to the lounge, to such an extent that Betty asked, 'What on earth have you two been up to? You look like you've swallowed all the cream.'

Daisy began to doze and Rufus appeared from whichever room he and his father had been occupying. Honey smiled at him, the incident of the other evening forgotten in her joy at her mother's pleasure. She put out her hand to pet Ruff before kissing Daisy on the cheek and going outside. The walk was vigorous and exhilarating and Honey and Rufus were both flushed by the time they got back to the Grange. Rufus put his dog in the back of the car and turned to say goodbye.

'Let's hope Ruff's had enough exercise to sleep through,' Honey said, unintentionally reminding them both of their previous meeting. *Is that an added flush to his face? Maybe he's regretting the abruptness of his departure last time.* Whatever it was, Rufus kissed

Honey on her forehead. In spite of her height, he needed to bend his head to do so. He was a tall man, though not as tall as Guy — and it was of Guy she was thinking as Rufus drove away.

'Would you like me to walk you home?' came a familiar voice.

Talk of the devil. Honey turned to greet him, the well-known smile giving her more pleasure than a whole afternoon had with Rufus.

'I'd like that, Guy. Yes, please, if you have time.'

'I'll always have time for you, Honey.'

She was startled — not at the words, because they could have been said light-heartedly; but at their intensity. Guy was no longer smiling and Honey, in an effort to calm her nerves, took his arm in sisterly fashion and said, 'Shall we?' Unfortunately the sisterly arm she'd put through his didn't feel like that at all and, when he took the hand she'd threaded through, her fingers tingled.

'Okay, I'll race you from the gate,'

Guy said, remembering she was some-one else's girl. 'Like when we were kids.'

'Your legs are a bit longer than mine now. It'll hardly be a fair contest.'

'I'll give you a start then. Go on. I'll count to five.'

By the time they got to the Honey Bun both were breathless and laughing — and completely at ease with each other.

★　★　★

Alexandra Ffoulkes, it seemed, had undergone a personality change. She became accommodating and pleasant to such an extent that Guy wasn't at all sure he didn't prefer the earlier version. At least he'd know where he stood with her then. He didn't trust his mother in this new guise although, as he hadn't trusted her before, there was no change there. But now he didn't know how to behave around her. No way could he be the affectionate son she suddenly seemed to want, but his innate kindness wouldn't allow him to shun her completely.

'Won't it be wonderful if it all goes through?' She'd found a cottage which, it seemed, was perfect for her. That in itself was a miracle. 'We can have Sunday lunches together. I'll be able to organise roast dinners just the way you like them.' Guy was at a bit of a loss to know how she came to be aware of his preferences, as she'd never taken any interest in the past. He was also sure that the said roast dinners would not be prepared by her own sweet hands, but the very fact that she was ready to organise them at all spoke volumes.

'I shall be delighted if everything goes smoothly, and of course it will be lovely to have lunch with you occasionally.' There was no way he was going to commit himself to anything regular — not that he thought she'd be able to keep it up anyway. 'If progress continues the way it has, we ought to be able to complete in three weeks.'

'I can't wait to get into my own place. They've been so kind at the hotel — Was this his mother speaking?! — but it isn't the same, is it?'

'How is the major? Have you seen him recently?'

His mother displayed a coyness that made him feel slightly squeamish, but he pushed the feeling away.

'Three times a week, sometimes four. And he's such a gentleman. Your father was never so solicitous.' Guy frowned and she had enough sense at least not to continue in that vein. 'So many years I lived in this area, and there's so much I've never seen. You should get out a bit yourself,' she suggested, not appreciating that her lack of parenting skills when he was a child might have had a lot to do with his current lack of knowledge of his home patch.

'Well I'm delighted you're enjoying yourself, Mother. You'll have to forgive me; I need to get back to see the construction manager.'

It was a lie, but a kind one, and no

one was more astonished than Guy when his mother said, 'Yes, of course. I understand,' when he knew full well she'd been hoping he'd stay longer and in the past would have made that perfectly clear. 'The major will be here soon. He's taking me for a spin.' *Ah, that would account for it then.*

★ ★ ★

Guy was back in the foyer at the Grange talking to Betty when Rufus pushed his father through on their way to one of the lounges.

'So when *are* you going to bring Connie and the girls? A man has the right to see his own grandchildren, doesn't he? It's been months.'

Rufus looked around guiltily but didn't see Guy and his manager, as they were in a large alcove that turned the area into an L-shape and were hidden from view.

'It's difficult, Dad. The distance; school; and then the children are always doing something at the weekend,' they heard him say as the two men disappeared through the doorway.

Guy and Betty looked at each other in silence for a moment, both shocked at the revelation. She was the first to speak.

'Well I never! Who'd have believed it, a nice man like that!'

'Obviously not such a nice man. I wonder if Honey knows.'

'Of course she doesn't! What's the matter with you, Guy? Do you really think she'd be seeing a man who's married to somebody else?'

'They may not be married. They could have divorced. That wouldn't stop Derek wanting to see them.'

'He'd have told her though. Guy, he'd have told us. He was ready enough to tell us about Ruff. And you saw how guilty he looked when Derek asked him about them. No, he's married all right, and he's making sure he has the best of both worlds. You have to tell Honey.'

'*Me?* Oh no, I couldn't.'

'I never took you for a coward, Guy Ffoulkes.'

'Then you were wrong. It'll be my fault for not knowing all the relevant details about the residents.'

Betty had to acknowledge the probable truth of what he was saying. 'Yes, she'll be that upset and I can see you might be in the firing line. But someone has to tell her.'

'You're right. Someone does. It just isn't going to be me.'

23

Easter arrived and brought with it the annual Rotary Club float. Mary Simpson and her teachers had done a great job with the children of Rills Ford, and if there were some slightly unusual costumes this year nobody minded. It's possible that somewhere in the universe there are rabbits with green fur and a marsupial's pouch (one of the mothers had joined in the fun and needed somewhere to carry her newborn). Naturally the baby's big sister had to have a duplicate. Then there was William, who came dressed as an archaeopteryx with the epithet 'Dino Saw' written on his back, and who spent his time wrestling with the biggest chocolate egg anyone had ever seen clutched in his wings.

The whole town turned out for the parade, and relatives and volunteers wheeled or supported those residents of the Grange who were fit enough to take part. Rufus was not there. He'd told Honey he was travelling that week and wouldn't be able to make it back. The pavement on the Honey Bun's side of the road was filled with trestle tables bending under the weight of their produce. Such was the goodwill in the town that most proprietors had left pricing labels and a dish for the money so that they too could join in the festivities. And the sun shone. Honey smiled as she pushed Daisy's wheelchair past her own table. It was always one of the first to empty.

'A person's got to eat, haven't they?' Mrs Worthington asked defensively as she purchased her second piece of cake just as Honey and Daisy were passing.

'Chocolate fudge cake,' Daisy said and pointed at the paper plate her friend was holding and whose contents were threatening to wobble off onto the pavement.

'Coming up,' said Mrs Worthington,

buying another piece and placing it precariously in Daisy's lap.

'I think maybe we'd better stop for a minute and put it on the edge of the table. Here you are, Mummy.' Honey handed Daisy a spoon already laden with cake and was delighted when her mother managed to raise it to her mouth without dropping it, using her once-useless but now improving hand.

The day was a huge success and the scouts and guides did a great job of clearing up after it was all over. Suzie doubled up as the paper's photographer, and a fine selection of pictures appeared in the next edition with the champion of the fancy dress contest winning a year's supply of chocolate, at which his mother said, 'I don't know whether to be pleased or horrified,' until she was told that what it actually meant was one chocolate button per day; and nobody was going to overdose on that.

★ ★ ★

The next time Honey visited her mother she was in high spirits. It was something she couldn't really put her finger on but it seemed Daisy was much more her old self — the way she'd been before her fall; the way she'd been when Honey's father was still alive. She remembered when Lucy and Basil were visiting; how much better Daisy had been with them, and even more so with Tom. She was pretty sure that all the external stimuli had made the difference, and that the Easter parade outing had been particularly beneficial. It made her think. It made her think very hard. *Was I wrong about change? Will the new building be the disaster I've always thought? It'll be a very different change from an outing or a trip to the Honey Bun; but those changes were beneficial, so why shouldn't this one be?*

Honey was filled with remorse. She'd been so quick to condemn Guy. And if the building was unfit for purpose — something she'd only learned recently — wouldn't the upheaval of a renovation have been even more unsettling than a straightforward move to another place? She went in search of Guy to apologise but instead ran into Mrs Worthington in the foyer.

'I just popped in to see your mother and we had a lovely time chatting to Derek Thornberry. He'd brought his photo album in to show us because Rufus had given him some pictures of his grandchildren.'

'I didn't know Rufus had a brother or sister,' Honey said, looking interested.

'As far as I know he hasn't. Why would you think that?'

Honey felt a shiver go through her. 'They're *his* children, the ones in the photos?'

'So I understand.'

'I wonder why he never told me he was divorced.'

'What makes you think he's divorced?' Mrs Worthington said as gently as she could. Everyone knew Honey had been seeing Rufus.

'Well, I . . . oh no! How could he?

261

Just wait till I see him.'

Fortunately Honey's temper overtook her dismay, and it was a very angry young woman who went in search of Rufus's father.

Happily, common sense had asserted itself by the time Honey ran Derek Thornberry to ground. She didn't have far to go. He was out in the garden and, as luck would have it, on his own.

'Hello, Derek. The garden's looking lovely, isn't it? How are you today?'

'As well as can be expected for a man of my age and a lot better than most, thank you.' He smiled. He had a charming smile, completely open, and Honey couldn't and wouldn't believe he was complicit in his son's deception.

'So how come you've ended up here, at the Grange? I believe you lived with Rufus before you came.'

'That's right, I did. But it was all a bit too much for my daughter-in-law, what with the little ones as well. I miss them, though. Them most of all. I don't think they've been to see me since I came, but that won't be their fault. She's never really been interested in me. I think she only tolerated me for Rufus's sake.'

'I'm sure that's not true,' Honey said, bowing to the inevitable truth. 'You're always such fun to be with.'

'It's kind of you to say so, my dear, and I do try. It's difficult not to be upbeat with so many nice people around. But you know what? I'm happy here. I'm not made to feel I'm in the way, and in some small part I'm able to help some of the others, those who are not quite as able as I am.'

'Well, you certainly cheer my mother up, that's for sure. In fact, if I didn't know better I'd think you were flirting with her.'

'My flirting days are over, Honey. I'm not as young as I was, not like my son.'

And that was the only indication she had that Derek might have some idea that she'd been involved in some small way with his son.

* * *

Honey left Derek in the garden and ran straight into Guy, literally. He was coming in through the front door as she entered the foyer.

'I'm glad to have bumped into you, Honey,' Guy said, smiling at his own joke. 'I know you're never going to forgive me but I'd like you to come and see the new building. It's really taking shape now and I'm hoping you'll be able to see how much better the facilities will be than they are here.'

He led her across the grounds and she had to concede that the buildings she thought would be an eyesore fitted in beautifully with their surroundings.

'It's still a hard-hat area,' he said, handing her one, 'but it'll be finished soon and I wanted you to be the first to see that I'm not being high-handed; that all I want is the wellbeing of those in my care.'

Honey could find no argument other than the old one about change; but as change was inevitable, if the licence wasn't going to be renewed then this

was certainly a purpose-made building
. . . and it had a soul. She could feel it
the moment she went inside. Guy spent
some time explaining the details to her.
He was so obviously proud of his
project.

'How are people going to be able to
afford to live here? It must have cost
you a fortune.'

Guy was wrong-footed and he knew
it. It was time to come clean. 'They
won't be paying any more than they are
now. Less, in fact.' He turned to her
and took both her hands in his. 'I don't
know if I can make you understand,
and I don't want you to share this with
anyone. Certainly not Suzie. It's my
way of giving something back, Honey.
Not everyone had the start in life that I
did.'

'That's for sure,' she said with a hint
of irony.

'I'm not talking about Alexandra,' he
replied, not even pretending to misun-
derstand. 'I was born into a wealthy
family, but most of what I have I made

myself.' She could hear the pride in his voice. 'I have more than I can ever hope to need. Care of the elderly has become an obsession with me, and this is not the first of what I hope will be many projects — but I don't want it put around. As far as the rest of the world knows, this will be run as a commercial venture. Betty knows, of course, but I wanted to share it with my best friend.'

Honey didn't quite know how to deal with this. She tried for a bit of light-heartedness. 'Well, it's certainly been a day of revelations. I've not long found out that Rufus is married with two children. How's that for a bolt out of the blue?'

'I'm glad you've found out. I didn't know how to tell you.'

'You knew? You *knew*! And you didn't tell me. How could you?'

'I thought you'd be hurt and I couldn't bear that.'

'Oh, and I suppose you thought it would hurt less if I found out later when I'd really become involved.'

266

Sarcasm is a useful tool sometimes, especially for women.

'You weren't involved?'

'No, of course I wasn't. We were just friends; at least, I thought we were.'

'Then you're free?'

Honey heard the hope in his voice. 'Yes, Guy. I'm free.'

'No, Honey, you're not,' he said, sweeping her into his arms. 'If I have my way you'll never be free again.'

THE END

We do hope that you have enjoyed reading this large print book.

Did you know that all of our titles are available for purchase?

We publish a wide range of high quality large print books including:
Romances, Mysteries, Classics
General Fiction
Non Fiction and Westerns

Special interest titles available in large print are:
The Little Oxford Dictionary
Music Book, Song Book
Hymn Book, Service Book

Also available from us courtesy of Oxford University Press:
Young Readers' Dictionary
(large print edition)
Young Readers' Thesaurus
(large print edition)

For further information or a free brochure, please contact us at:
Ulverscroft Large Print Books Ltd.,
The Green, Bradgate Road, Anstey,
Leicester, LE7 7FU, England.
Tel: (00 44) **0116 236 4325**
Fax: (00 44) **0116 234 0205**

GRACIE'S WAR

Elaine Everest

Britain is at war — but young Gracie Sayers and her best friend Peggy are determined they will still have fun, enjoying cinema trips and dances with Peggy's young man Colin and her cousin Joe. However, there is something shifty about Joe, and Gracie finds she much prefers Colin's friend, the kind and decent Tony. Then, one night, a terrible event changes everything. Now Tony is away at war — and Gracie is carrying the wrong man's child . . .

CUPCAKES AND CANDLESTICKS

Nora Fountain

When Maddy's husband Rob suddenly announces that he's leaving her and moving to Canada with his pretty young employee, her world comes crashing down. As Rob's promises of financial support prove worthless, Maddy finds herself under growing pressure to forge a new life for herself and her four children. She decides to start a catering business, but will it earn enough money — and is that what she really wants? And then she meets the gorgeous Guy in the strangest of circumstances . . .

FLIGHT OF THE HERON

Susan Udy

On her deathbed, Christie's mother confides to her daughter that she has family she never knew existed — grandparents, a great-aunt, and an uncle — and elicits a promise from Christie to travel to Devon to meet them. When she arrives, she's surprised to find another man living there: the leonine and captivating Lucas Grant. But when her grandmother decides to change her will and leave Christie a sizeable inheritance, it's soon all too evident that someone wants to get rid of her, and both her uncle and Lucas have a motive . . .

THE DAIRY

Chrissie Loveday

Georgia is the rebellious eldest daughter of George Wilkins, managing director of the family business, Wilkins' Dairy. Studying for a degree in art, she has become involved with a fellow student, Giles. Following lunch with him and his eccentric artist mother, she ends up moving in with them — but finds it hard adjusting to such a dramatically different lifestyle. Meanwhile, George is struggling with difficulties of his own at the dairy. Can father and daughter both deal with their troubles and find contentment?

A WHOLE NEW WORLD

Sheila Holroyd

Marla's attempts to become an actress and model have stalled. While she decides what to do next, she goes to live in her dead uncle's house in the country, with its tantalising clues to his mysterious past. Then comes an unexpected chance to restart her modelling career — but if she seizes this opportunity it will mean abandoning the new life she has made for herself, and not only new friends but also a possible romance. Which should she choose?

THE THREE-YEAR ITCH

Liz Fielding

It has been three blissful years since Abbie married Grey Lockwood. She has it all: a glamorous jet-setting career, a beautiful home and, best of all, a loving husband to come home to. Her friends tease her that they would never leave a man as devilishly sexy as Grey on his own for long, but she always thought their marriage was based on trust. Yet . . . has she left Grey alone once too often? He no longer seems satisfied with a part-time lover. He wants a full-time wife — *any* wife!